RARE

BETH YARNALL

RARE

ebook ISBN: 9781940811871

print ISBN: 9781940811536

1

Erin sat at her aunt's bedside, holding the hand that had wiped her tears, braided her hair, and waved to her from their front porch everyday as she came home from school. She didn't know what she and her father would have done without Aunt Cerie. She'd come into their lives and everything that lay between Erin and her father had been put to rest.

Her parents' growing arguments had dotted Erin's days and nights with paralyzing dread, relieved only by bouts of guilt. She'd lie in her bed night after night, listening, knowing what was going to happen and unable to stop it. She'd *seen* it. Late one night, two months shy of her eighth birthday, Erin had awoken to the muffled sound of her parents' shouting. When the startling, terrifying silence came, she curled into a ball, squeezing her eyes shut. She knew her father was standing in the open doorway, watching her mother's taillights fade into the distance. He'd cried. Erin hadn't.

Aunt Cerie had arrived a few days later and had never left. And now here she was in a hospital bed, her eyes jittering back and forth beneath her eyelids, her breath catching and hitching in her chest. She owed her aunt so much. Cerie let out a fretful sound, the kind a frightened child makes, and her hand jerked from Erin's. The alarm on the machine next to the bed suddenly went off, jolting Erin to her feet.

Erin did the only thing she could think of, she gripped Cerie's hand and reached out with her mind, not knowing if her aunt could hear her or not. *I'm here, Auntie. It's okay. I'm right here. Everything's going to be all right.*

After a moment, Cerie settled in the bed, but her eyes still darted back and forth beneath her eyelids.

A frazzled-looking nurse bustled in and pressed a few buttons, putting an end to the noise of the machine. She flipped through papers on a clipboard. "Looks like we'll have to increase her dosage," she said.

"Dosage of what? What's wrong with my aunt?" Erin asked, trying to keep the fear from her voice.

"I'll send the doctor in to talk with you. He's just finishing up with another patient."

"Thank you."

"Are you okay?" The nurse asked, pointing to her own nose. "You're bleeding."

Startled, Erin touched a finger to her nostril and it came away red. It was getting worse.

"Here." She handed Erin a box of tissues. "You better sit down. Apply pressure. Don't tilt your head back."

Erin did as instructed. "Thank you," she mumbled around a wad of tissues.

"I'll send the doctor in to speak with you shortly."

Erin continued her silent ramblings, which seemed to soothe Cerie considerably. She wasn't as agitated as she'd been when Erin first arrived. Erin focused her thoughts, keeping them positive. After a few moments, her nose stopped bleeding so she went into the bathroom to clean up. When she came out, a doctor was at her aunt's bedside, listening to her chest.

He looked up as Erin came into the room. "Hello. I'm Doctor Frost." He took the stethoscope out of his ears and slung it around his neck, then gently raised Cerie's eyelids, shining a light back and forth.

"I'm her niece, Erin."

"Can you tell me about what's been happening with your aunt?"

What could Erin say? That her aunt was a mind reader? That someone was messing with her ability? All of their abilities. That her aunt didn't have the same defenses as she and her father and that's why she was so affected? "She's been having severe head pain off and on."

"When she came in, she was nonresponsive." He flipped up the blanket covering Cerie's feet, took out a wheelie thing and rolled it over her the contours of her foot. "She's not responding to pain. Has she had an accident? Maybe a fall?"

"No, not that I know of."

"Is she on any medication, prescription or otherwise?"

"No. Absolutely not."

"Does she have a history of migraines or high blood pressure? Seizures? Mental disorders?"

"No. None of those. She's always been healthy."

The doctor felt her aunt's scalp, her neck. "No signs of trauma. I want to run some tests. Mostly neurological."

Erin didn't ask what the doctor was looking for. There was nothing in this hospital that could help her aunt. "Is she...suffering?"

He straightened and looked at Erin. "We've got her under sedation. She was quite agitated when she first arrived."

"But is she in any pain?"

"To be honest, I'm not sure. She's not responding to the medication as she should, so I've prescribed a higher dose sedative. I'm concerned about her heart. Is there a history in your family of heart disease or high blood pressure?"

"No. What's wrong with her heart?"

"Her blood pressure is elevated. We've given her some medication to help bring it down, but again, it isn't having the effect it should. Can you think of anything that could have caused this? Any changes in her life or lifestyle?"

"Sorry. No."

He nodded and consulted the chart he held in his hand. He scribbled down some notes, then flipped it shut and headed for the door. "We'll keep a close eye on your aunt."

"Thank you." Erin watched the doctor leave, then

turned to her aunt. "You've got to calm down, Auntie. You heard the doctor." She slipped Cerie's hand into her own. "I don't know what's happening to you... to us, but I'm going to find out."

Her aunt shifted in the bed.

"Graham's here. He knows, Auntie. He knows all about my ability. I'm helping him find out what's happening."

Cerie's body stiffened and her heart rate went wild on the monitor.

"Auntie, please calm down. It's all right. Everything's going to be okay." Erin flicked a nervous glance from her aunt to the monitor and back again. She didn't know what she'd do without her aunt. Worry crawled inside her and weaved its web, wrapping her chest in tight bands. Erin couldn't lose her. She wouldn't lose her. She'd do whatever it took to stop whoever was doing this to them. Whatever it took.

GRAHAM STARED into Donald's eyes, chilled by what he saw. Donald was there, but inaccessible, as though he was looking at Graham from the bottom of a deep, dark pit.

"Tell me what's happening to you," Graham said.

Donald's gaze held firm as though he was trying to convey something he couldn't with words. "Happening," he repeated.

"He won't tell you anything," a voice said from behind him. Graham spun around to see Mabel, standing in the doorway. She made her way toward them, her eyes on Donald. There was a softness in the look she gave him and an extra sway in her step. "He hasn't been able to do much more than repeat words or phrases for days now." She settled into the chair next to Donald and patted his shoulder.

"What are you doing here?" Graham asked.

Mabel smoothed the hair that Donald had plucked at back down over his ear. "Erin and I have been taking turns looking after Donald and Cerie." She turned her cunning gaze on Graham, brows raised. "I could ask you the same question, Sheriff."

"What do you make of Donald's and Cerie's...conditions?" he asked, avoiding Mabel's question, at the same time, feeling disrespectful talking about Donald as if he weren't sitting inches away.

"I think..." She stopped Donald from reaching up to pull at his hair again and twined his fingers in hers. "They're in trouble."

Graham had to tread carefully here, unsure how much Mabel knew about the December family's abilities especially Erin's. "How so?"

"Isn't it obvious?" She leaned across Donald and whispered, "Evil's taken up residence in San Rey."

"What do you mean, evil?"

"Witches," she breathed.

"Witches." He pressed his lips flat to keep from laughing out loud. *Was she serious?*

"It's the only explanation. They've put a spell on San Rey. All the crimes...the murder...you can't tell me that's not the work of sinister beings."

Graham sat back in his chair. She was dead serious. Witches. "Is that why half the town has horse shoes tacked to their front doors?"

"Witch repellant."

"Well, it's not working. And just how did the town come to believe witches are causing all the problems?"

Mabel's gaze slunk to the corner of the room. "Everyone knows Samhain is their high holiday."

"Mabel," he began to admonish, then decided against it. Let the town's people believe what they wanted. It wasn't like he had a better explanation for what was happening. "You haven't seen the witches, have you?"

She scooted to the edge of her chair, her full focus back on Graham. "As a matter of fact—"

"Mabel." Erin approached them. "I didn't realize you were still here."

Jumping to her feet, Mabel dropped Donald's hand as though it was a live grenade. "Of course, dear." She approached Erin, a blush blooming from her chin to her hair. "Have you seen Cerie?" She wiped her hands on her hips. "Of course you have. How's she doing?"

Graham stood, too, with the growing realization that Mabel, the most gossipy woman on the planet, had a secret she didn't want revealed. Interesting.

Erin crossed her arms, rubbing herself as though she were cold. "She's sedated. They're going to run some tests on her."

"Does the doctor know how to help her?" Mabel asked.

"He thinks it might be some kind of neurological problem." She hitched her shoulders. "I don't know."

Erin looked so lost, so alone. Graham wanted to go to her and put his arms around her, but not with Mabel the Mouth standing right next to them. What was building between him and Erin was too fragile, too new. He felt an overwhelming need to protect it, to protect her. She'd only just broken up with Keith a few short hours ago. The gossips would spin that against Erin and she didn't deserve any more of their hate.

"Witches," Mabel whispered behind her hand to Graham.

"It's late. Why don't I take you and your father home?" he asked Erin.

"I don't know." Erin's gaze roamed the room. "Someone should stay with my aunt."

"You should go home, dear," Mabel said. "Get some rest. Cerie wouldn't want you to make yourself sick over her. I'll take Donald in to see Cerie and then home and to bed."

"Good idea," Graham said, looking to Erin for agreement.

Erin mulled the suggestion over, then nodded. "All right."

Erin said her goodbyes and they were on their way. She was silent on the elevator ride down to the parking garage and as they made their way to Graham's car. He helped her in and then slid into the driver's seat.

Erin spoke as they hit the freeway. "Will you stay with me tonight?"

He jerked the wheel, nearly crashing into the car next to them.

"I don't want to be alone," she finished in a rush.

Her face was turned away from him so he couldn't be sure of what exactly she was asking. He adjusted his hands on the wheel and swallowed hard. "If you want me to."

"I—" She shook her head. "Thank you."

"Sure."

After a moment of quiet in which a thousand questions bounced off the inside of his head, he asked, "Could someone be...doing this to you and your family?" As far fetched as it seemed it was the only possible explanation as to what was happening.

"I think that's a strong possibility. The attacks—and that's the only way I can describe them—feel deliberate, targeted. Controlled."

He could only nod. He was so far outside the realm of his experience here. He'd been trained to think in black and white, absolutes, tangibles. What was happening to Erin and her family was anything but that. He let the thought that a person could be responsible for the attacks—as Erin had called them—flow through him. His mind wanted to reject it, but the more he considered it the more possible it seemed.

She picked at the seam of her jeans. It made a tick, tick sound like the countdown of a clock. They drove farther, leaving the stars and the moon behind them, the night sky blackening as they drew closer to the coast. The storm brewing over the open water would be upon them well before morning came. Cold warning licked up his spine. He repositioned his hands on the wheel, resisting the urge to fold Erin's hand into his. Things were about to get a lot worse before they got better. This town was seriously fucking with him. He'd never had premonitions before—didn't believe in them —but he couldn't seem to stop the rumbling sensation of a boulder full of bad shit barreling their way.

"He's targeting our specific abilities," she said, her voice hollow. She startled a glance out of him and he found her watching him, as though judging how much more he could take. "Turning up the volume," she continued. "So Aunt Cerie hears every thought of every person around her as though they were screaming. A constant, never ending barrage of noise. I don't know how much more she can take.

"And my dad... he's losing the ability to communicate. Not just putting thoughts into people's heads, but verbalizing. He's slipping away. From life, from reality..."

"From you?"

"Yes."

"How many people know about your power? I mean really know."

"We call them abilities," she corrected. "They're a skill, not a tool."

"Ability, then. Who knows about them?"

"My dad, my aunt, you...my mom."

He remembered the gossip around town about Colleen December. And when she'd walked out on her husband and child. Her name, whispered like a curse, had been on everyone's lips. Even now, years later, her name sparked hushed conversations and shaking heads. Instead of putting the blame where it laid—on Erin's mother—the talk turned toward Erin and speculation that there must be something wrong with her or else her mother never would've left and not looked back.

"When was the last time you spoke to your mother?"

"Doesn't matter. She wouldn't be involved."

Graham pondered her strange choice of words—wouldn't be involved. "Maybe she told someone."

"She doesn't tell people about me."

That surprised him. He wanted to know more but she was already changing the subject.

"I've worked really hard my whole life to keep my ability a secret."

"Even from friends and boyfriends?"

"Until recently it's been an easy secret to keep. I had control over the visions or at least control over when and what I saw. Now they come at me out of nowhere and it's getting harder for me to climb out of them."

"So you can call up a vision about a particular person or event. Specifically?" he asked.

"Yes."

"How?"

"All I have to do is concentrate on a person, decide if I want to see the past or the future, and then bam, I see it."

Did she have visions about him? Did she know about what had happened in L.A.? He wanted to ask, but didn't really want to know the answer. Something else nagged at him. "Do the people you have visions about know? I mean, can they feel it?"

"Not as far as I know." But he could hear the uncertainty in her voice.

The obvious question lay between them so he asked it, "Can you call up Deidre's murderer again, maybe see his face this time so we know who we're dealing with?"

"No."

"No, as in you tried and couldn't or no, you won't?"

"I tried, but there's a...block. I don't know how to describe it. I don't know who he is so I can't access the vision that way. When I tried going back to the day of Deidre's murder there's nothing to grab onto. It's blacked out."

"You said you can feel your dad and aunt in your head and purposefully block them. Is it possible for someone with another kind of ability to know when you're using your ability on them?"

"If they can, they've never told me."

"*Would* they tell you though? I would think that would give them an advantage they'd want to keep to themselves."

"How very cynical," she accused. "Is that what you would do with your own family?"

"Probably not, but with anyone else—"

"*Anyone* else?"

"Most anyone else. Look, I'm just trying to work through how whoever's manipulating your family's abilities is able to target each of your specific talents. And how they seem to know about your secret ability."

He exited the freeway and turned onto the two-lane

highway that led to the center of San Rey. Lightning flashed, illuminating Erin's face for the briefest moment. Even with the frown creasing her brow, she was so lovely, his next breath stalled in his chest and he had to force his focus back to the road ahead.

"I don't know," she finally answered. "I just don't know."

He reached for her hand and found it clenched in her lap. She resisted at first, then relaxed, slipping her fingers into his.

"I'm sorry," he said, offering useless words instead of pulling the car over and clutching her against him, as he really wanted to do. "I know none of this is easy."

"That's my life...not easy."

Her laugh, full of worry and fear, fisted his gut. He held onto her tighter and pressed a little harder on the accelerator. They came over a rise and the lights of San Rey sparkled in the distance as the first raindrops hit the windshield.

"How long have Mabel and your father been seeing each other?" he asked to shake loose the mood that had settled over them like the storm clouds outside.

Her laugh was real this time. "Close to ten years. They think no one suspects."

"Seemed obvious to me."

"My aunt and I have known for years, but pretend we don't. I think they like the illicitness of their off and on affair."

"Wasn't she still married to Calvin Hobbs up until a couple of years ago?"

"She married Calvin when she and my dad were in

an off phase," Erin said. "She does that when she gets mad and frustrated because my dad won't marry her. Breaks up with him, marries someone else, gets a divorce and then takes up with my dad again."

"Why won't your dad marry her?"

"He's still waiting for my mom to come back," she answered quietly.

"Do you think she'll come back?" he asked, just as quietly.

"No. Never."

"You've seen it." He didn't have to ask, he just knew. "But you haven't told your dad."

"No. We don't talk about her."

"I'm surprised he's never asked."

"He had his chance to make her stay and he didn't."

"By using his power, you mean? How would that work? He puts the thought in her head that she should stay with him and then what?"

"Why not? What good are our abilities if we don't use them?"

"What kind of victory would that have been?"

"Victory?" She tried to tug her hand free, but he wouldn't let her.

"You know what I mean. He would always know that she stayed because he forced her to, not because she wanted to be with him."

"And what about me?"

Her question threw him. He suddenly had an image of Erin as a child, growing up with rumors and pitiful glances instead of her mother. Maybe. Maybe if he were in Donald's place he'd have used his ability to spare his child. Everything in him immediately argued against that thought. He'd just as soon wait out the rest of his life, as Donald had, for a wife who was never coming back than live with the artificiality of a forced relationship. He'd always know, in every look, every show of affection that none of it was real. And it would shame him.

"Maybe if he'd made her stay she might've gotten past...things," Erin said. "And I wouldn't have had to grow up without her."

"It's no different than using your visions of the future to alter it. Just because you have an ability doesn't mean you should use it every chance you get."

"You sound like my aunt."

"Cerie's a very smart, very scary woman."

"Are you saying that if you had an ability you'd never use it?"

He hitched a shoulder. "Depends on the ability."

"What if you could move objects with your mind and you saw that a little girl was about to be hit by a car. Would you use your ability to save her? Or would you stand there and watch her die?"

"I..."

"It's not so easy, is it?"

"Change one thing and you could change everything."

"The Butterfly Effect. I know. I live with it. It's like if I'd done something about seeing Greg dead. Stopped it somehow. I would have altered everything that came after. Like this moment, this conversation. None of it would have happened. To be honest, sometimes I don't think changing things would be such a bad idea."

"Have you ever?"

"Changed things? I tried once. With my mother. It obviously didn't work out. Now the fear is too deeply ingrained. In that way, Aunt Cerie did a phenomenal job raising me."

"I'd say she did a phenomenal job all the way around."

He pulled up to the police station, cut the engine, and turned toward her. He could just make out her features in the dim streetlight. Lightning flared, illuminating them both for the barest of seconds. Thunder rumbled low as he reached for her. She met him halfway and he was finally, finally kissing her. Being with her, kissing her pushed everything else away. It was only them. Him and her and nothing else.

"I lied earlier," he said, breaking the kiss to trail his lips along her jaw line.

"Hmm?"

"I lied. I would've saved that girl from the car. Or at least tried."

"I know."

It was such a relief to hear her say that, to know she believed in him. Maybe he wasn't so lost after all if she could find him amongst all the horror of what they were up against. He recaptured her mouth, pouring every grateful thing he felt with her into one kiss, one long, slow caress. She clutched at him, matching his urgency with hers.

His thoughts scattered, spiraling into a single need,

sharp enough to slice him in two. He struggled to remember where they were. Struggled to right his world and put her, this kiss, and everything else into some kind of perspective. But when they broke apart and he looked into her eyes, he saw everything he was reflected back at him. She'd scrubbed him clean of his past and presented him back shiny and new and worthwhile. He wanted to be all of that for her. All of that and more.

"Erin," he begged.

"Ssh."

"I don't think I can do this." He wasn't the man she thought he was. She didn't know the shit he carried around and how much of that would get piled onto her. He couldn't do that to her.

She put a hand on his cheek and leaned in close. "I know."

2

They left his car in front of the police station and walked up the hill in the rain to Erin's house. Standing at her door, dripping, Erin struggled to fit the key in the lock. She shook, not from the chill, but with a craving that ran so deep, it scared her more than anything. If Graham were going to reject her, she'd just as soon he did it right here on the porch. Once they crossed the threshold she couldn't be responsible for what she might do. Desperate as she was, she wasn't above begging and that, well, that would be the end of whatever they had going here and the last of her self-respect.

He fit his hand over hers and guided the key into the lock for her. She turned it and hesitated, biting the inside of her cheek. He put a hand on her shoulder, twisting her around to face him. The last shreds of her control slipped away under the heaviness of his stare. She saw the same mixture of longing, nerves, need, and unworthiness she felt.

She fisted the front of his shirt and pulled him through the door with her. She didn't stop pulling him until they were in her bedroom. There, they squared off. And then he slowly reached back and closed the door behind him. In the darkness she could feel him, burning in the space between them. She didn't know who moved first, but suddenly they were on each other, kissing, touching, yanking at clothing, each other's and their own.

His shirt hit the floor with a wet smack. He'd gotten soaked, having left his coat with her father. That thought did more to excite her than the magic he was doing with his fingers and mouth. And oh, what magic it was. Her blouse and bra vanished, replaced with his hands. He bit her earlobe and she let out a loud moan, her knees dipping. His chuckle was low and wicked as he bit her again.

"God, Graham."

"Yes, Erin?"

"You're wearing too many clothes," she panted, reaching for the button of his pants.

"So are you," he said, shoving her jeans down her hips.

He cupped her backside, bringing her up against him. She could feel the hardness of him and renewed her efforts to free him. The wet denim wouldn't budge. She made a frustrated noise, which seemed to amuse him as he took over the job, slipping out of the rest of his clothes faster than she could have wished them away.

The first feel of him skin on skin nearly pushed her

over the edge. He groaned and pulled her closer, pressing against her belly. She ran her hands over him, learning the lines of his body. The hardness here, the fleshy tautness there. She skated her fingers across a puckered ridge on his side. The anomaly drew her back to it, but before she could explore it further, he captured her hand and brought it to his chest. He turned them, moving them toward the bed. She tripped, her feet tangled in her wet jeans. They fell together in an ungraceful heap on the floor. She landed on top of him, hitting her forehead on his teeth.

"Ow!"

"Damn it!"

"Are you okay?" they asked in unison.

She buried her face in his chest and laughed. His chuckle reverberated against her cheek.

"That wasn't the seduction I had planned," he said after a few moments, humor in his tone.

"You *planned* to seduce me?"

"Planned. Fantasized. Daydreamed. Night dreamed. Thought about it every moment of every day."

"Seriously?" *Seriously?*

"I'm a guy."

She adjusted her position, purposefully rubbing against him to tease. "I noticed."

With a growl, he rolled them. "Hmm, what else have you noticed?" he asked, brushing the hair back from her face and smoothing a thumb over her forehead where she'd injured herself. He kissed it.

"I've noticed that your beard is softer than it looks."

To prove it, he glided his chin back and forth across the top of her breast. "What else?"

"You feel good. All over."

He ran a hand over her shoulder, down her arm, brushing across one breast, dipping in at her waist and around her hip, sliding down her thigh then up between her legs. "So do you," he murmured. "So soft. And wet."

"Also," she gasped, widening her legs for him. "I noticed... uh... oohhh... yes... there... oohhh... yeesss... the f-floor."

"The floor?" he mumbled around her nipple.

She reached down and cupped him. His breath quickened, blowing hot on her skin. She stroked him once, twice...

"It's hard," she rasped.

"Mmm." It seemed to take him a moment to get her meaning, then his head came up and he released her nipple with a pop. "The floor, you mean."

"That too."

He leveraged himself off her and pulled her upright by the hand. She tried to stand, but was hampered by her pants around her ankles. They both worked to get her free, finally realizing that she was still wearing her shoes. He tugged too hard, scooting her bare backside across the carpet. She yelped at the burn and he dropped her foot free of the shoe, which came down in his lap. He curled up, half laughing, half grunting in pain. Out of her clothes at last, she moved to try to help him.

"I'm so sorry. Are you okay?"

"Yeah, but a kiss would make it better."

"Is this part of your seduction plan?" she chuckled. "Because I have to tell you, your skills could use some work."

"Is that a challenge?"

"Only if we move to the bed."

"Race you there."

They scampered up off the floor and dove for the bed, collapsing into the pile of pillows she had stacked up. Graham pulled at pillows, tossing them aside, until he found her laughing up at him. He looked down at her with a naughty grin that made every part of her keenly aware of him, especially her too long neglected parts.

He bent his head and kissed her, gently, as though this alone was all he wanted. She shifted beneath him, accustoming herself to his weight and the way they fit together. Sliding his hands into her hair, he deepened the kiss. Her body became heavy, languid in the first flush of desire. She shifted again and he settled between her legs, right where she most wanted him. Groaning, he ground against her. She brought her knees up and slid her feet up his legs, locking him to her.

Rocking her pelvis, she brought him right to her entrance. All he had to do was push into her. He was right there. So close. He pulled back, moving away from her. She made a noise of disappointment and followed him, using her feet to bring him back to her.

"God, Erin... I can't... I'm—"

She reached for him between their bodies. He

gripped both of her hands suddenly and pinned them above her head.

"Stop doing that. I can't take—" His words ended in an incomprehensible grumble as she once again pressed her pelvis up, bringing him against her once more.

She thought she'd die without the feel of him inside her. She wanted him now, hard and fast. No gentleness, nothing slow or deliberate. She wanted a mindless coupling, a crude fucking. There'd be time for finesse later when the need wasn't so sharp. As if hearing her thoughts, he held her hands in one hand and slipped one, then two fingers inside of her, testing.

"Do it," she commanded. "Do it now."

"Stop it or I won't last two seconds."

"I don't care."

"That's what you say now," he murmured in her ear, stroking her. "I want you screaming as I pound into you. Over and over." He quickened the pace as she writhed against his hand. "Harder and harder. I want you to yell my name when you come."

Her breath came in short pants. She was so close. He nipped her earlobe, then sucked on it. But she held back. She wanted him with her. He held her hands tight and whispered naughty things in her ear, all the things he'd do to her. She struggled against his hold. Even though she could, she didn't break it. Her resistance brought her body in constant contact with his. Her whole body was on fire, burning to join with his. He coaxed her on. The filthy things he promised drove her mad as erotic images played one after the other behind her closed eyelids.

Her loud gasps filled the room, nearly drowning out his words as he drove her wild with his dirty mouth and skilled hand. On the threshold of orgasm, she sucked in a stunned breath as he suddenly replaced his hand with his cock, pushing hard into her. Gripping the sheets, she came long and loud, shouting his name. He rocked into her once, twice and then he too reached his climax, muffling his groan in her neck.

His breath puffed against her heated skin, scattering goose bumps. She'd wanted mindless. What she'd gotten was earth altering and embarrassing. She squeezed her eyes shut, reliving the way she'd wantonly begged him to screw her, then got increasingly hotter at the dirty, almost disgusting suggestions he'd whispered in her ear. Is that what he thought of her? Did he think she wanted him to do all of those things to her? Her cheeks heated as she remembered the particular scenario he'd been filling her head with when she came.

She tried to disentangle herself from him, but he was still inside her. At her movement he stirred, sliding deeper into her until he hit her most sensitive spot. He pulled out, then in again, still hard within her. She attempted once more to get out from under him, but he gathered her to him.

"We did it your way, Babe," he whispered. "Now we'll do it mine."

He stroked into her, nearly all the way out, then deep. His movements were languid and deliberate as though he were learning her from the inside out. Her body reacted, flushing hot. Pleasure rippled through her. She ran her hands over his sweat-slickened body, down his back, clutching his bottom as he seated himself deep. The play of muscles beneath her hand thrilled her so much she moved to grip both cheeks as he plunged into her once more.

Smoothing her hair back, Graham kissed her as he'd intended to from the start, taking his time. But the tension was already building, pushing at him to plunge hard and fast into her. Sweet Jesus, the sounds she made. She wasn't quiet in her pleasure. He was quickly learning which touches brought her to the edge. How his mouth could make her squirm and the surprisingly naughty side of her that had shocked them both. He liked it all. He'd barely made it into her before it was all over for him. He'd take his time this go around and wouldn't let her push him.

But even as he made the vow, she gripped his ass, her nails sinking into his flesh. Her cries urged him on, yanking on the leash of his control. Everything she did, every sound, every movement was maddening. He could have her a thousand times and never experience all the ways in which she could drive him wild. He picked up the pace, sweating with the effort to last longer this time. Bending his head, he sucked her nipple. She rocked into him, meeting his thrusts. But she held back.

He hit into her harder, faster. Her screams filled the

room and yet she held out. He hooked an arm through her leg, then the other, pushing her into the bed. He'd meant to go slow, but she'd challenged him. Her pleasure was a goal he chased now with a single-minded determination that blotted everything else out, including his own impending orgasm. He fused his mouth to hers, muting her cries. Their panting and the hard slap of flesh on flesh filled the silence.

And then she broke, her back arching. He stiffened, his own release crashing into him. Releasing her legs, he collapsed down next to her. His mind blank, his heart pounding, he sucked in air. The room came into focus inches at a time, beginning with Erin's face, which was turned away from him. The long line of her neck beckoned for a kiss if he could only move. His gaze drifted down to her breasts, rising and falling as she too regained her breath. He'd had fantasies about those breasts. None of which he'd gotten to fulfill. Damn it.

"You have control issues," he said. Or at least that's what he'd intended to say. Only it came out more like *Thew haff conthrol isthues* as he still couldn't quite feel his tongue.

She turned toward him. "Is this more of your crappy seduction technique? Actually, I guess it would be your post seduction technique."

"My technique is not crappy. It got you off. Twice."

"Hmm... Well," she hedged.

"I never would have pegged you for a screamer." He grinned at her, stupidly pleased with her and, not to brag, himself as well. "A dirty girl, too."

"Shut up."

He chuckled and followed her as she tried to move out of his reach. With his lower body still pinning her to the mattress, she didn't get far.

"I liked that too," he said, nuzzling her neck.

"You're a degenerate."

"Hmm, maybe. I had to really stretch to come up with some of that stuff though."

"Not that far."

"No, not that far. I'm going to do some of that stuff to you, you know," he said, circling her nipple with the tip of one finger.

She swatted his hand away. "I'm not interested."

But she broke out in goose bumps, her nipples tightening, giving away just how interested in some of that stuff she really was. His dick twitched at her reaction. With more encouragement like that and some time, she'd have him hard and ready for yet another round. He grinned at her.

"You're very pleased with yourself."

He shifted to lie next to her, yawning. "No, just you."

She rose from the bed. He stacked his hands under his head and sighed, watching as she padded to the bathroom, her violin curves pale in the moonlight. Erin was his. He shouldn't feel guilty about that. So why when he closed his eyes, still smelling like Erin, did Patricia's image come to haunt him? He tried to push it away. Put it back in the box of things he didn't want to look at. But instead of Erin's curling brown hair and toffee colored eyes, he saw Patricia's long black locks and deep brown eyes. And why, when he inhaled, did

Erin's light scent mix inexplicably with Patricia's heavy perfume?

He pressed the heels of his hands into his stinging eyes. The thought of her still got to him even now, months later, in another woman's bed, fresh from another woman's body. Patricia was always there at the fringes of his consciousness, like the scar on his side, a constant reminder of his failings.

Erin came back to bed and slipped in beside him. He wrapped himself around her, breathing her in, trying to chase away the demons of his past. Lethargy blanketed him, heavy and warm. But even as he felt the tug of sleep, the specter of shame called him what he was...murderer.

GRAHAM KNELT BY THE BED. The morning sun set the room aglow, casting soft light over Erin's prone form. She lay on her stomach, face turned toward him. Her curls spread out around her. Unable to resist, he smoothed back the lock that lay across her face. Her nose twitched. He hated to leave her, but he'd put off questioning her ex-boyfriend too long. For her. He'd much rather strip back down and slip into bed beside her. Maybe make love to her once more.

He leaned over and kissed her cheek, then the hand that hung off the edge of the bed. Her lashes fluttered and then she nailed him with her very direct stare.

"Hey," he said, caressing her cheek with the back of his finger.

She leveraged up and turned, tucking the sheet around her. "Hey."

"I have to go." He didn't want to tell her the reason and bring the outside world into the space that had been theirs. He'd already brought too much in and would have to find a new way to deal with that.

"Oh." She seemed to catch his meaning anyway with her one word response.

"Do you want to have dinner with me tonight?"

"I don't know. I have to check on my dad and go back to the hospital."

Awkwardness hung in the air between them, an end of the first date kind of nervousness. "I'll call you."

"Okay," she said, doubt leaden in her tone.

"Erin..." he started, caught by the look in her eyes. He found he couldn't finish. Everything he thought to say sounded trite and overused. Instead he dropped to his knees, wrapping his arms around her, and kissed her. He put the words he couldn't say, the feelings he couldn't express into this one kiss. How much he craved her, how much he needed from her, how much he wanted to give her, and how much he wanted to take away from her. How much he wanted to be in her body, her thoughts, her life.

He broke the kiss and stumbled to his feet, gripping the bedpost for balance. "I'll call you," he said again, his voice raspy and raw sounding.

She put the back of her hand to her mouth and nodded. "Yes. Call me. Come over later if you can."

"Okay."

"Okay."

He turned and left, concentrating hard on putting one foot in front of the other when all he really wanted to do was dive back into bed with her.

ERIN WATCHED HIM GO, her heart hammering, her stomach a tangled knot of excitement and need. Damn, that man could kiss. At the sound of the front door closing, she flopped back in the bed, snuggling down deep in the covers. She'd think about that kiss all day with the same goofy grin she wore now.

Her senses stuttered, flashing like a warning light. And then she was sucked out of her bedroom and into another room with bare, hard-worn furniture. A woman lay on the floor, her dark hair obscuring her face. Erin could hear voices down the hall, arguing. Another woman... no a man, his voice high and tight, yelled something about what he was owed. A deeper voice answered, his tone low and cajoling, promising the other man that he'd get what he was after.

The woman on the floor stirred as one of the men came into the room. He leaned over her, his bulbous belly making the task seem herculean, and kicked her. She jerked and curled into herself. The man bent to kick her again, but the other man—Graham—came into the room, stopping him with one word—"Don't."

Graham argued with the fat man over the woman as if she were a commodity he was trying to unload at a good price. Erin stood invisible at the edge of the room, trying to make sense of what she was viewing. This was a Graham she'd never seen before, hard-edged and clean-shaven, his beard gone, his hair shorn close to the scalp. He was keyed up, eager to get the fat man to agree to the deal. The woman tried to get his attention, but Graham ignored her, focusing on the other man. The man took the deal with the caveat that the woman would leave with him. Graham didn't hesitate, quickly agreeing. The woman glared hard at Graham and tugged on his pant leg. Graham shook her off, stepping away.

The fat man smiled down at the woman, saying something in a language the woman understood but Erin didn't. Rising to her feet as though she were in a lot of pain, she answered back. Whatever she said earned her a backhand from the man that sent her sprawling to the ground again. Graham shoved the man's shoulder, getting in his face. Behind the men, the woman slipped a gun out of her boot. She aimed it at Graham's back.

The explosion hit Erin as though she'd been the target. The room flashed white. Erin sucked air...once again back in her bed. The morning sun filtering into her window a mockery of the horror she'd just seen. She pulled the pillow Graham had used to her chest and hugged it hard. It still held his scent. She'd allowed the vision to go on further than it should have. She'd wanted to know more about Graham. Was that how he'd gotten the scar on his side? The one he'd tried to hide from her.

The Graham in her vision was not the Graham she'd had in her bed last night. She tried to reconcile the two in her mind, comparing them side-by-side. If he could slip so easily from one persona to the other, which was the real one? Or was the real Graham caught somewhere in between? And who was the woman in the vision? There'd been moments Graham had looked at her with real emotion when the fat man hadn't been paying attention. Who was she to Graham? Did she have a claim on him still?

3

Graham had gone home to shower and change. He'd grabbed a cup of coffee and a donut at the Do or Dine and now he stood on Keith's doorstep, wondering if he'd missed the man. He didn't want to have to question Keith at the store with half the town straining to listen, didn't want any more of this to touch Erin in any way.

It was just a matter of time before the whole town knew he'd spent the night with Erin. He should have left earlier. When he'd turned around to start down Erin's front steps, old Mrs. Pfeiffer had been standing on the sidewalk holding her bug-eyed mutt's leash, gaping at him as though he'd just climbed out Erin's bedroom window with her panties clamped between his teeth.

He'd given her a wave and a cheerful *mornin'*. She'd given him a glare that let him know his father would be hearing about this. His father had strict beliefs where premarital relations were concerned, not to mention the six generations deep worth of reputation to protect.

Goddamned small town.

He banged his fist on the door harder than necessary. "Keith! Open up. Sheriff."

No answer. He looked up at the two-story house that gleamed with a new paint job under the morning sun. This might've been Erin's house one day. It was perfect for her, in the kind of neighborhood where you'd raise a family. She might've had the life here with Keith that she'd wanted, if things had gone differently. He gave the shiny silver plate at the bottom of the front door a solid kick and was about to turn away when he heard a crashing noise from inside.

He hit the door with his fist, annoyed with himself as much as Keith. "Open the door, Keith!"

Silence. He tried the doorknob. Locked. He shook his head and muttered a curse as he stepped off the porch. All the peeping in windows he'd done lately was going to earn him pervert of the year status. The house was dark and still feeling. He had no idea what room he was looking into. He knocked on the window and shouted for Keith again, then skulked around to the side yard. Another window, drapes shut tight.

He opened the gate, letting himself into the backyard. More family home goodness here with a swimming pool, basketball hoop, and a freaking swing set. All that was missing was the dog. As soon as he had the thought, a big shapeless mutt bounded toward him, tongue lolling. The dog bounced around his ankles until Graham found a ball and threw it. The dog followed, disappearing into some bushes, leaving the ball on the grass.

"Not so perfect after all, huh?" he muttered. "Dog can't even fetch."

The back of the house was locked up as tight as the front, the curtains and shutters closed. He made his way to the front of the house again and was standing at the bottom of the steps, deciding what to do when Carol Whittaker came up next to him.

"Have you knocked?" she asked.

"No answer."

"He didn't come in to work today. Not answering either of his phones. Maybe we should be at Erin December's house. I hear things have gotten pretty serious between them. Although I don't know what he sees in her. He could do better."

Graham tamped down his anger. "They broke up."

Carol looked at him funny. "That can't be right."

He shrugged, looking back at the house, feeling as though it were looking right back.

"But they had a date last night. He was really nervous like something big was going to happen, if you know what I mean."

"He didn't call in to work or anything?"

"No, not a peep, which isn't like him. That's why I came down here. As assistant manager of the pharmacy."

"And you haven't been able to reach him? What about his parents?"

"He's not there either."

Graham strode up the front steps and pounded the side of his fist against the door. "Keith!"

"The key's under the mat."

"Of course it is." Graham lifted the corner and retrieved the key.

"Should I stand back? Is this police business? Do you think something's happened to Keith? Maybe he's sick. Or fell down and hit his head. He could be lying unconscious, bleeding to death slowly."

Graham glared at Carol over his shoulder.

"Well, he could. Happens all the time."

He fit the key in the door and opened it. "Sheriff. Keith, you in there?" He turned back to Carol with a hand up. "Stay here."

He made his way through a short entry hall into a main room with a wide, sweeping staircase. The second floor overlooked the first with an open floor plan with a vaulted, beamed ceiling. Keith hung limply, suspended in midair from one of the beams. Face ashen. Neck cinched. Head jerked off center.

Dead.

"Goddammit."

Behind him, Carol shrieked. Graham ducked at the onslaught. She stood there, mouth opening and closing on one scream after another, eyes wide, finger pointing. He clamped a hand over her mouth, but she howled through his fingers as he pulled her back out the door.

"I told you to stay outside!"

Her wailing continued, her arms pumping up and down at her sides.

He gripped her shoulders and shook her. "Stop it! Stop it right now!"

She shut off mid screech. Her chin quivered. Tears filled her eyes. They poured over her bottom lashes, spilling down her cheeks.

"Goddammit," he muttered, noticing the doors opening up and down the street.

"He's-s-s de-e-ad."

"Yeah."

"D-d-do s-s-something."

"Come sit down." He guided her to his car and put her in the front seat. "Will you listen to me this time and stay put?"

She nodded, swiping her hands over her face. "I have to call the store."

"No. No phone calls. I mean it." Graham eyed the Looky Lou's who were gathering, leaving their lawns to come see what the fuss was all about. He pulled out his cell phone and called Pax.

He answered on the first ring. "Riggs."

"Pax, we've got another unattended death."

"Jesus. Another one? Who?"

"Keith Collins."

"Are you shitting me?"

"I wish," Graham answered. "And I'm going to need some crowd control."

"I'll take care of it."

Graham ended the call in time to be surrounded by neighbors, clamoring for answers.

"Everyone step back," he ordered. "Go back to your homes."

"Why's Carol in your car?" someone shouted.

"What'd you do to Carol?"

"Carol, what's going on?"

"What's happening?"

"Keith's dead," Carol announced, collapsing into sobs.

The crowd sucked in a collective breath, then pelted Graham with a thousand questions at once, like a swarm of mosquitoes each trying to take a bite out of him. He did his best to control the crowd and managed to stop one morbid neighbor, the McGuire's oldest son, from sneaking into the house.

By the time Pax arrived with a couple of other deputies, the crowd had Graham backed up against the front door and wondering for the millionth time why he'd come back to this godforsaken backwoods town where everyone knows everyone and they all knew way too much about each other's business. Seeing Graham's predicament, Pax put two fingers in his mouth and let out a whistle. The crowd quieted.

"Now, give the sheriff a chance to do his job," Pax said. "You all go back to your homes."

"If he was doing his job we wouldn't have so many people dyin'," someone shouted.

That started a tidal wave of *that's rights* and *yeahs*.

"Give the boy a chance."

Every head swiveled to see the newcomer who defended Graham. The crowd parted and Ham came into view. Graham bit back a curse. This was just what he needed. A dead man, a mob of angry neighbors, and now his dad. Ham leaned heavily on the cane he'd used when he'd first come home from the hospital. Graham knew the fact that Ham had conceded his need for the cane meant that he probably should've been in a wheelchair. Sweat beaded Ham's forehead and although his hand shook as he raised it to point at Graham, his back was straight. Damn stubborn old man.

"That there is the sixth Sheriff Doran of San Rey," Ham said, his voice strong but strained. "He's here to do his job. Go on back to your houses and let him get on with it."

There was some murmuring and hard stares, but one by one, the neighbors all went back to their front porches and windows to watch the comings and goings at Keith's house. When the last straggler finally wandered away, Graham rushed to his father's side to help him sit down on the front step.

"You shouldn't be here, Pop."

"You should be thanking me, not scolding me. Where's your respect?"

"Sorry, it's just— " Graham spotted his father's car parked across the street. "You *drove* here?"

Ham pulled a handkerchief out of his pocket and dabbed at his forehead. "I can drive just fine."

But he couldn't walk the four blocks from his house to Keith's.

"Pop—" Graham started, then realized he had three deputies waiting for orders. "Deets, start the log. Smith, keep anyone who isn't wearing a uniform out of this house. Send the coroner in when he gets here. Pax, with me."

Ham struggled to his feet. Graham considered sending him home, but the firm set of his father's mouth told him he'd better not even try. So, Graham helped him up the steps.

"You're an observer," he told Ham.

Ham waved him off. "No touching. Got it."

They took off their hats and made their way into the house. Keith's body was the same as Graham had left it. Now that he could examine the scene without an air raid siren screeching in his ear, Graham noticed a few things he hadn't the first time he'd been in the room. Keith was missing a shoe. It lay a few feet away near the couch. A lamp had been knocked over, the shards of broken light bulb glimmered like strewn confetti across the hardwood floor.

The knot under Keith's jaw pushed his head to the side. He looked just as polished, just as perfect in death as he had in real life. Erin had told Graham how upset Keith had been. How panicked and cornered he'd behaved when she'd confronted him about his affair with Deidre. Could Keith really have had something to do with Deidre's death? Was the baby she'd been carrying his? Had he killed himself instead of owning up to his affair with Deidre?

More than anything, Graham wished he didn't have to tell Erin about this on top of everything else she was dealing with.

Pax whistled. "That's a long way up. How do you think he did that?"

"There's no ladder," Graham responded.

"Second floor balcony." Pax nodded. "Why do you think he did it?"

"Could be because my son, the sheriff, is having... relations...with Keith Collins' girlfriend."

Pax's gaze swiveled from Graham to Ham, then back again.

"Pop—"

"Is this true?" Pax asked.

Ham glared at his son.

Graham shifted his feet under the condemning stares of the two men he respected most in this suffocating small town. "They broke up."

"You need to get your act together." Ham pointed at Graham, his face mottled. "Unmarried. Cavorting with that...that December woman. Trash. All of them."

"Don't talk about her like that," Graham warned, closing in on Ham.

"You're jeopardizing your legacy. Our legacy." Ham shook his head and wobbled a little. "I understand a man's need, but find a woman of quality. Or find what you need outside of town."

"I did what you wanted. I came back here and became sheriff. I'm not going to let you or anyone else tell me who to spend my time with."

"Don't you dare speak to me like that! You don't tell me, I tell you." The force of his statement sent Ham back a step. Graham reached for him, but Ham moved away, wiping a trembling hand over his mouth. "I may not be sheriff anymore, but I'm still your father."

"Gentlemen—" Pax began.

Graham interrupted, "I care about her. And nothing you say will keep me away from her."

"I won't have a December bastard for a grandchild!" Stumbling, Ham came up against the doorway. He struggled for breath. Clutching his chest with both hands, his cane clattered to the floor.

"Pop!" Graham rushed to his father's side. Pax helped Graham ease his father to the floor. "Call an ambulance," Graham ordered.

"No." Ham gripped the lapel of Graham's jacket. "Promise me you'll stop seeing her."

"Pop, you're sick. You need to go the hospital."

"Promise me."

The panic that squeezed Graham's gut spread, constricting his lungs until he thought he'd vomit. He couldn't do it. He'd done everything Ham had asked, but he couldn't do this. Staring into his father's eyes, he couldn't lie to him either. "I'm sorry."

Pax mumbled into his phone. Graham's pulse thundered in his head. Outside, birds chirped, a dog barked. In the distance, the ocean rumbled low, a sound so constant it was white noise. Through it all, Ham's words rang sharp as a bell though he only whispered. "You're no longer my son."

"You don't... Pop..."

Ham turned his face away, releasing his grip on Graham.

"An ambulance is on its way," Pax said.

Graham backed away, looking down at the man who'd been his hero his whole life. He'd done everything, *everything* his father ever asked of him. But it was never enough. Ham asked for more, always more.

Pax knelt down next to Ham and unbuttoned his collar. He was saying something to Ham, but all Graham could hear was the roar in his head *You're no longer my son. No longer my son...*

"Graham."

Pax's voice broke through. How long had Pax been calling him? He slowly pulled his gaze from his father to look at Pax.

"He's going to be fine. Don't you worry," Pax said.

"Sure."

"Why don't you go with him to the hospital? The guys and I can take care of things here."

"Yeah. Okay."

"Graham, I'm going to need to talk to you later. And Erin too. Get your statements. Your whereabouts. Considering everything. It's just a formality."

"Whatever."

"He's going to be fine," Pax repeated.

Graham nodded, edging out of the room that suddenly felt overly hot and stifling. He broke out of the house as if he'd been forcibly expelled, running down the steps to his car. Carol still sat in the passenger seat with the door open.

"Go home," he told her.

"But you said—"

"You can go."

"All right." She climbed out of the car, eying him warily. "Are you okay?"

He slammed the car door shut. "I'm fine."

"What should I tell everyone at the store?"

"Tell them what you want. That's what everyone else in this town does. Why should you do different?"

She gave him a look of hurt before she turned to walk down the hill back into town. He watched her go, guilt coating over the sickness in his stomach. He'd told her he was fine. He wasn't. He wasn't anything.

Who was he if he wasn't Ham Doran's son?

4

Erin watched the lines and numbers on the machine next to her aunt's hospital bed, willing them to even out as her aunt's heart rate spiked again. The sedation helped, but didn't minimize the intermittent twitching and stiffening of Cerie's body. She was worse than she'd been the day before.

Erin finished reading the last paragraph of the chapter in the book she'd found in her aunt's purse, and set it aside. She'd attempted to reach out to her aunt mentally all morning, trying to soothe her, but she couldn't seem to get past the barrier caused by the medication or whoever was manipulating Cerie's ability. Reading the book aloud had been a futile act of desperation. She may as well have been reading to the wall. Erin rose and stretched. She sniffed back the tears that had been threatening to spill over every time she looked at her aunt's still, pale form. She needed a walk, a change of scenery, something.

She came out of her aunt's hospital room to find

Graham leaning against the wall. Her pleasure at seeing him was quickly replaced by alarm at the look on his face. He pushed off the wall and without a word, wrapped his arms around her, burying his face in her neck.

"Graham, what's wrong? What's happened? Is it my dad?"

He pulled out of the embrace and smoothed her hair away from her face. "No. God, I'm sorry. I didn't mean to scare you."

"But something's happened."

"How's your aunt?"

"They've put her in a medically induced coma. She's... What's wrong?"

"Not here."

He took her hand and led her down the hall. She thought he'd take her to a quiet hallway or waiting room, but they turned a corner, then another to a room marked *Private*. He towed her into the room, closing and locking the door behind them. Backing her up against the door, he pressed his body to hers and kissed her. He smelled like the outdoors, breathing in his scent, her body responded. His desire fueled hers. She kissed him back with equal fervor as though there wasn't enough time, enough skin on skin, enough of anything to ease the restless wanting.

She didn't understand what was happening or why. Even if she wanted to, there was no time. He already had her bra undone, his mouth moving down her neck. She tilted her head back as he slid a leg between hers, pressing hard against her.

"I need you," he whispered, his voice hoarse and pleading, his hand bunching up her skirt.

She plunged her hands into his hair and brought his mouth back to hers. She was on fire, burning with a need that seemed to rise with his. Her thoughts fled, scattering to the wind at the feel of his hand there, just there. She welcomed the oblivion, falling further under his spell. She squeezed her eyes closed, heightening the sensations that barreled into her. There was only him, the feel of him and a need so consuming she forgot where she was. He was everywhere and yet not where she needed him most.

He pulled her panties aside, pushed one finger in, glided out, and replaced it with two. She slid down the door, her legs widening. He caught her around the waist, covering her mouth with his to silence her cries. He stroked her until she clutched at him, desperate for the feel of him inside her, filling her. And then he was there, pushing into her, gliding deep. He held onto her, driving into her, his tongue mimicking his thrusts.

She came hard, her scream muffled by his mouth. He pushed her down onto him as he hit deep. Burying his face in her neck, he shuddered, groaning as his orgasm slammed into him. Pinned to the door by his body, she went slack, her body quaking in the aftermath. She struggled to even her breathing, loose limbed and completely spent. He kissed the side of her neck, her jaw, then her mouth. Gentle open-mouthed kisses. Cradling her face in his hands, he set his forehead to hers.

"I'm sorry." His words whispered across her lips.

It took her a moment to make out what he was trying to say. "You're sorry?"

He pulled out of her and lowered her to the floor. Brushing the backs of his fingers over her cheek, he looked like he regretted what they'd just done. "This wasn't... I didn't come here for this. I'm sorry."

She adjusted her underwear and smoothed down her skirt. He watched her movements as he, too, righted his clothing.

"What did you come here for?" she asked, afraid of the look in his eyes. She didn't know if she could take any more bad news.

"Let's sit down." He put his arm around her shoulder and led her to a small leather couch. He sat close, his arm still around her and reached for her other hand. "I have to tell you something."

"Just say it."

"Keith's dead."

She jerked as if he'd hit her. Keith...dead. "What? How..."

"Suicide."

She tried to bolt, but he held onto her. "No." She shook her head, unable to wrap her mind around what Graham was saying now. Something about hanging. "He wouldn't. He just wouldn't. Not Keith. No." She pushed at his hands, fought to get free. He released her and she bounded off the couch. "I don't believe you." She turned back to him and could see it written across his face as though he was seeing a scene she couldn't. "I don't believe you."

"I'm sorry."

"Stop saying that!"

He stood up. "Keep your voice down."

"You didn't care about that when you were shoving my skirt up."

"Erin—"

"How could he be dead?"

He reached for her hand, squeezed it.

"He's too perfect to be dead." She looked up into Graham's face, could see there was more. "What? What aren't you telling me?"

"Pax has to question us."

"We're suspects?" The hits just kept coming. "I thought you said he killed himself."

"He did. It's a formality."

"Wait. Why does he want to question *you*?"

He pulled her into him. She let him, needing his strength.

"Pax knows about us," he said, rubbing her back.

The insinuation sank in, bringing with it crushing dread. "Everyone's going to know. They'll think..."

He brought her head against his chest. "Yeah. I know. I wanted you to be prepared."

She pushed against his chest, out of his arms. "Prepared? They're going to blame me for Keith's death. I break up with him, take up with you, and the next day Keith kills himself. How in the hell do I prepare to have the whole town hate me? They'll think I'm a whore. Oh, God." She fisted her hands in her hair. "Oh, God." She bent over. "I think I'm going to be sick."

"Erin. Babe, don't." He took her by the shoulders,

pulling her upright. "Don't blame yourself. It's not your fault."

"I'm not upset because I blame myself, you idiot. Keith couldn't have cared less about me. He didn't do this because of me. I know that. If anything, he did it because of you."

He looked surprised. "Because of me?"

"He knew you were going to question him about Deidre."

"You think he killed her?"

"No... I don't know." She threw her hands up, paced away, then back. "Actually I do know. Keith didn't kill Deidre. It wasn't him I saw in my visions. Graham, this is bad. This is really, really bad."

"What do you mean?"

"I think he might have known who killed Deidre. Or at the least, suspected."

"Why?"

"He was afraid, panicked. He knew you were going to question him, but I don't think he was afraid for himself. What if he knew who killed Deidre and was killed because of it?"

"Erin, the house was locked when I got there. I saw no signs of a struggle."

"I could use my ability. Focus on Keith and maybe I'll get something—"

"No. It's too dangerous."

"Why not? Last time I used it I was fine. This could give us the break we need to solve Deidre's murder and Keith's, too."

"Erin, stop it. Just stop." He reached a hand out to her, his voice gentling. "Come here."

She looked down at his outstretched hand. It blurred. She blinked, her vision watery. "I'm not crying."

"Okay."

"I never cry."

"I know, Babe. You're very brave." He stepped closer. "Come here."

She fell into his chest and he held her. Tears slipped down her cheeks, wetting his shirt. He bent over her, seeming to need the contact as much as she did. Sighing, he snuggled her closer. She fisted his shirt, trying to get a hold of herself. Why was she crying over Keith? She didn't love him. It was all just too much, she guessed. Her aunt, her father, Deidre, Greg, and now Keith. What was happening with her ability? Not to mention the hot sex with Graham. He'd scrambled her brain and made her want things. Turned her world upside down.

And yet here he was, so strong and sweet. He drew her in closer, hugging harder as if he needed her just as much as she needed him. Maybe more.

"Graham?"

"Hmm?"

She pulled back to look up at him. "There's something else you're not telling me."

"My dad's down in emergency."

"What? Why aren't you with him?"

Pressing his lips together, his gaze moved to a spot just beyond her ear. "They're running tests."

"Is he going to be okay? What happened?"

"He'll be fine. Why don't we get a cup of coffee or something?" He released her and moved toward the door. "Maybe lunch."

Something was off with him. "Graham, stop. Tell me what's really going on."

GRAHAM WASN'T ABOUT to tell her the things his father had said about her. She'd been through so much. He shoved his hands in his pockets and looked at her, really looked. Her face was flushed, her eyes overly bright. He wasn't going to add to her worries especially with the problems she'd been having with her ability. *Her ability.* Damn it.

"Did you say you'd used your ability without a problem?" he asked. "When was this?"

Her eyes went wide. "What?"

"You heard me."

"You must have misheard me." She shifted, jutting out her chin. "Why are you changing the subject?"

He folded his arms across his chest. "Why are *you* changing the subject?"

They stared at each other across the small room, squaring off. He was for damn sure not going to tell her about his father and he could see she wasn't going to confide in him about her latest vision. So where did that leave them?

Her gaze skidded past him to the door. "I should go check on my aunt."

He cleared his throat. "I should probably check on Pop."

They didn't move.

She looked around the room as if noticing it for the first time, taking in the small couch and chairs, the generic pictures of nature. "What is this room?"

"Grieving room for families."

"Oh, my god. We had sex where people grieve for their dead relatives?" She wrapped her arms around herself and rubbed them, shuddering. "That's...not right."

His eye caught on a portrait of Jesus and he shook his head. "It's really not."

"What are we doing here?"

Her tone sent his heart stuttering. She was looking at him, waiting for an answer as though he might actually have one. As though he could put two coherent thoughts together when she looked at him like that. The only thing he knew for sure was that she was too far away and too near. He could smell her, that faint tropical scent so uniquely her. He could feel her, her essence, her emotions, her uncertainty. He could almost taste her, remembering how perfectly their bodies fit together. What *were* they doing here?

Already they were headed for disaster. If he had a brain in his head he'd end this, do what his father wanted, spare Erin what would surely be hell for her. All she'd wanted was to fit in with this stupid town and now Keith's death, combined with her involvement with Graham would probably ensure that never happened. The people of San Rey had small minds, big mouths, and long memories. There would always be whispers about how Keith had killed himself because she cheated on him with Graham.

If it was even possible to stop it. By now he'd bet half the town already knew about them and about Keith. The damage was done. All he could do now was try to cushion some of it for her, be there for her. He didn't kid himself into thinking his motives were entirely selfless. They weren't. He'd always been a self-serving bastard. Why should that change? Especially with her feet away, still waiting, still looking at him, expecting things from him.

"We're...figuring things out," he answered lamely.

"When do you think we'll have them figured out?"

"I don't know."

She nodded at that. "Okay."

"Do you think it can be figured out? I mean, is it possible?" he asked.

"Yeah, I kinda do. Don't you?"

Suddenly everything was set right. He smiled. "Yeah."

She smiled in return, tilting her head a little to the side. She was so damn pretty he couldn't stop himself from touching her, reaching out to stroke her cheek with the pad of his thumb. So soft. She eased into the caress, her lashes lowering. He leaned in to kiss her. How could he have thought of ending things, ending this? He framed her face in his hands and deepened the kiss. She moved into him, gripping his wrists. He broke the kiss before things got out of hand. Again.

"You're very good at that," she said.

"At what?"

"Making me forget."

"At least I'm good for something. Do you want to go back to your aunt?"

She smoothed a hand over the wet spot on his shirt where she'd cried. "No, I want to go down with you to check on your dad."

"We can go down. See what his doctor says. But we probably won't be able to see him." No way in hell.

He didn't know what it would do to his pop to see him with Erin and he knew exactly what it would do to their fragile relationship if she found out his father had disowned him because of her. Family was everything to Erin and he knew she would rather break things off with him than get between Graham and his father.

"Oh, okay."

They headed down to emergency and found out that his dad was going to be admitted overnight for observation. Erin decided to go back upstairs to check on her aunt, leaving Graham with a kiss and an invitation to stop by her house later. Graham watched her until the elevator doors closed and she disappeared from his view. He turned to go see his father before they took him up to his room, wondering how he was going to sort things out with his old man.

Graham pulled back the curtain around his father's hospital bed and cautiously stepped inside. Ham pinned him with the dark-eyed stare he'd come to dread as a child.

"I've decided to give you another chance," Ham said, motioning for Graham to sit down. "But you'd better listen to me. You're going to shave your beard and get your act together. You're going to stop seeing that December girl. And you're going to start living up to your potential as a Doran and sheriff of this town." He shifted in the bed, sitting up straighter. "I've held off the mayor and his cronies from recalling you as sheriff, but I don't know for how much longer."

At first his father's words had given him hope, but then he quickly dashed them on the rocks of stubbornness. Graham reclined in his seat, settling in for what he knew was going to be a long lecture. "Have you?"

"I can arrange for you to make a speech. About how concerned you are, your plans for the town, that sort of thing. We can squash this."

"Can we?"

Whatever drugs they were giving Ham had a rejuvenating effect. If it wasn't for the weight loss and paleness Graham could have sworn his father had never been ill.

"But the town's going to want to see you're serious. Some outward indication," Ham said.

"Like shaving my beard."

"You're not in Los Angeles anymore. You're back here where you belong. Dorans have been trusted to keep San Rey safe for generations and we're going to keep on doing that. Your son—"

"What if I have daughters? Or no children at all?"

"Stop being flippant, Graham. This is serious."

"Pop, you're not going to want to hear this, but you need to. I'll make that speech. I might even shave, but the rest is none of your business. I get that you don't like Erin although I don't know why. I hope as you get to know her—"

"*Get* to know her? Oh, I know her. I know her kind. Beauty is temptation. Descended from Eve, women tempt men into sin. You must not let your lust for her deter you from your duty—"

"Her *kind*?"

"You can do better."

"No, actually I can't."

"She's twisted you around so you can't see clearly. I've been there, son. I know what it's like to be tempted, to partake of forbidden fruit. To be drawn in. It's enticing. Exciting. But you'll see I'm right soon enough."

"What's that supposed to mean?"

"Eventually she'll show her true colors. Your lust for her will fade and you'll see her for what she is."

"Stop hinting at it. Say it plainly, Pop. What exactly is she?"

"First Keith Collins and now you. He was a good man and if it weren't for her, he'd still be alive. Look at what's in front of you, son. Look at it."

"You can't be serious. You think she had something to do with Keith's death?"

"She traded a maybe for a somebody." He pointed at Graham. "You."

Graham stood. "I'm not going to listen to any more of this."

"Don't go against me." Ham leaned forward in the bed. "Or I'll make sure your little hussy is exposed for what she is. Her *and* her family."

"That's enough."

"I hear her aunt overdosed. A combination of pills and alcohol. She's right here in this hospital—"

"Not one more word about Erin or Cerie or anyone else I care about—"

"I might look like a weak old man, but I have more power than you know. Jobs dry up, leases get revoked, people fall on hard times, can't pay their bills." Ham waved a hand. "Happens all the time."

"You wouldn't."

"That's the thing about living in and serving the same small town for generations, people think they owe you."

"Why? Just tell me why you dislike the Decembers so much."

Ham leveled his son with a look that knocked him back to the days when he lived in his father's house and had to abide by his rules without question. Only those days were gone. And in the ensuing years Graham had learned to question everything, including himself. Especially himself. A lesson left over from the nightmare in L.A.

"I don't have to explain myself to you," Ham said. "Do as you're told."

If Graham had hoped to compromise with his old man, he knew now that option had never existed. Ham didn't negotiate. He set the terms and everyone else abided by them. He stared at his father, saw himself in the set of his jaw and the color of his eyes, and did the only thing he could—he went against his father for the first time in his life.

5

Erin arrived at her father's house just after dark, more exhausted than she ever remembered being. She let herself into the small cabin tucked into the hills above San Rey where she'd been raised. Following the sound of the television, she did her best to scrub the worry from her expression. There'd been no change in her aunt all day. Erin had left Cerie's bedside with little hope for her aunt's recovery.

She found her father in his recliner, staring blankly at the TV screen. The light from the television cast a sickly blue glow over his form, giving the scene a macabre feel. Kneeling next to the chair, she took her dad's hand. He turned toward her, his eyes burning bright in the darkened room.

"Hey, Daddy. How are you feeling?" No response. "Aunt Cerie is doing well." She stumbled on the last word and Donald's eyes widened a fraction. Or had she only imagined it? "Have you had dinner?"

"I fed him."

Erin jolted at the sound of Mabel's voice.

"Sorry," Mabel said. "I thought you knew I was here."

Erin squeezed her father's hand and rose. "You stayed with him all day?"

Mabel motioned for Erin to come back to the kitchen with her. Erin gave her father a sad glance and followed.

"Have you had dinner?" Mabel asked.

"No."

"Sit down. I'll warm up a plate for you. How's Cerie? I wished I could've come to the hospital to see her today."

Erin sat at the little dining table and filled Mabel in on Cerie's condition, watching Mabel navigate the kitchen as though she cooked in it every day, going straight to what she wanted without having to search. Which spoke volumes about Mabel's relationship with Donald. She couldn't help the tiny seed of bitterness toward the woman. It should've been Erin's mother sliding a plate of food in the microwave for her, not this placeholder in her father's life.

"He's worse, isn't he?" Erin asked about her dad, staring at the boomerang pattern in the Formica tabletop.

"Yes."

"How bad?"

Mabel hesitated, causing Erin to look up. Her expression said everything. Mabel had never been good at hedging. Donald had made a comment once about

Mabel's inability to keep her emotions from showing on her face. Something about the honesty of it and how he always knew where he stood with her. Erin thought the woman had never bothered to perfect her poker face so that people would ask her what was wrong and she could tell them the latest gossip with complete impunity. After all, they'd asked.

"He couldn't talk when he woke up," Mabel finally said. "Hasn't said a word all day. Just looks at me with his fevered eyes. I don't know what to do for him." She covered her face with her hands and burst into tears.

Erin sat there for a moment, uncertain. She'd never been close to Mabel. They'd been neither adversaries nor friends. Finally, she stood and went to Mabel. Stretching out a hand, she patted Mabel's shoulder. She couldn't help the slice of anger that stabbed at her. Mabel should've been consoling Erin. Not that she wanted the woman's pity, but it would have been a nice gesture. A bridge-gapping effort that could've gone a long way. Instead Erin stood there, comforting the woman who was her aunt's best friend and her father's off and on lover in the kitchen her mother had decorated.

"I don't understand what's happening," Mabel cried. "To Cerie. To Donald. This whole town."

"Me either."

"I wanted to take him to the doctor, but he made me promise not to. What am I supposed to do for him?" Mabel said, dabbing her face with the apron she wore. The apron Erin had given her mother that last Mother's Day. "I just want my Donald back."

"Me too."

"What could be causing this? It seems like that storm brought more than rain. It also brought trouble. For everyone."

"I wish I knew."

"Has your ability been affected?" Mabel asked, looking up at Erin through her lashes.

For a moment, time slowed and Erin imagined what it would be like to share her ability with Mabel, how freeing it would be. And she realized that maybe she didn't want to keep her secret anymore. Telling Mabel would be one way to reveal all, but was that how she wanted to break her silence after all this time? No. It was better this way, better to keep pretending she was as normal as everyone else, regardless of how they accepted her. She guessed it was all about what she could live with and the known evil versus the unknown.

"I don't have any ability," Erin said. "You know that."

"Are you sure? I always thought you'd grow into one. Donald told me how he came into his later, in his early twenties. I thought maybe... Well, I guess it's a blessing you don't, considering what's happening to Donald and Cerie."

"I suppose so."

The microwave dinged, prodding Mabel into action, wiping at her tears and fussing over the hot plate.

"Come and sit down." Mabel set the plate on the table and looked back at Erin expectantly.

Erin did as she was told, the aroma of beef stroganoff made her mouth water and she realized she'd hardly eaten all day. "Thank you, Mabel. It looks wonderful."

"You're welcome."

Mabel smiled and Erin thought maybe she'd judged her too harshly. Mabel sat across the table from her.

"I've never had a man kill himself over me," Mabel slid in easily, ruthlessly. "What's that like?"

Erin's fork clattered against the plate and her jaw dropped open, but Mabel went on as though nothing was amiss.

"I heard there was a suicide note, professing his undying love for you. You should probably speak at his funeral. People would expect it. Although I wouldn't wear black." Mabel leaned forward and whispered, "You weren't married, after all, just dating, right? But that's not the same." She sniffed back another tear, her gaze darting longingly to where Erin's father sat in the other room. "I should know."

Erin scraped her chair back from the table and started to rise, revulsion gnawing at her insides.

"Where are you going?" Mabel asked. "You've hardly touched your dinner. Oh, I'm sorry. I didn't mean to upset you. Please, sit back down." She waved Erin back. "I won't mention Keith again. You poor dear. Sit."

Erin eyed Mabel, then her plate. She was ravenous.

"Please sit."

Erin dropped back into her seat and picked up her fork, her gaze frozen on Mabel as if she was a viper poised to strike at the least provocation. She began shoveling food into her mouth as Mabel switched gears, gossiping about Jessica and the Billings boy, as Mabel called him. By the time Erin scooped up her last bite, Mabel must have decided that her window of getting anything out of Erin was quickly closing.

"How's Sheriff Doran senior? I heard they took him to the hospital."

"I don't know."

"You know, I always thought Keith was wrong for you. Now, a man like the current Sheriff Doran—"

"Thank you for dinner, Mabel," Erin said, rising. "I'm beat. I'll say bye to my dad on my way out." She paused, thinking that Mabel wasn't *all* bad, she just couldn't help herself. "Thanks for taking care of Daddy. I really appreciate it."

"Oh, well, of course. You know how I feel about your father."

"I do." And that was the only thing keeping Erin from wrapping her hands around Mabel's neck most days. "But thanks just the same."

Erin went back to the living room. Her father stared into the flashing screen at some sitcom. She bent and kissed his forehead. "Night, Daddy." He didn't look up.

Stepping out into the darkness, Erin breathed deeply, hugging her coat closed. The salty night air also carried the sweet smell of wood fires. The residents of San Rey would be huddled indoors, preparing for the coming workweek. A slip of paper under her car's windshield wiper caught her attention. She pulled it out and slid into the driver's seat, then immediately jumped back out of the car with a shriek.

A large crow, stiff with death, lay on her passenger seat.

Her heart banged against her ribcage as she slowly looked around. The street was deserted. There were few houses in this area of San Rey, mostly cabins built around the time the town was founded. Although the Decembers had been one of the first families to settle here, they'd never really been welcomed. Erin opened the note.

We're watching.

She scanned the street again. No movement. No maniacal face peeking out from behind a tree. No torch-wielding mob. Stuffing the note into her pocket, she took a deep breath and tried to shake off the eerie feeling that she *was* being watched. She pressed a hand to her forehead and tried to think what to do. Her lip trembled and she bit down on it.

She would not cry.

She climbed out of the car, marched around the side of the cabin to the shed in the back, and grabbed a shovel. Doing her best to not look too closely at the crow, she disposed of it. Someone *was* watching, she was sure of it now. Suppressing a shiver, she climbed back into her car and drove down the hill into town faster than she normally would. It was late enough that most of the businesses were closed. She passed Lucky's Bag N Save and saw that they flew their flag half-mast in Keith's honor. Several other homes and businesses did the same.

This sleepy little coastal town had been her home all her life. Now each quaint shop, every charming building seemed a charade. Which of the good citizens of San Rey had sent her that message? Who had let loose an avalanche of death and destruction that pitted resident against resident? What would San Rey become now that a serial killer existed among them? Because that's what he was. Erin was sure of it.

She pulled up to her house and parked. It was as she'd left it. She didn't know what she'd expected. Maybe another message. Maybe Graham waiting for her on the porch as he'd been waiting for her when she'd come out of her aunt's hospital room. Thinking of him conjured up memories of their night together. Remembering some of her favorite moments, she climbed her front steps and let herself in. She flipped on the lights and set her things down.

The pain struck like a hammer to a bell, reverberating in every cell in her body. At first she thought she really had been hit as she staggered into her living room, hands pressed against her temples. White-hot light filled her sight. She tripped into it, falling head first into the vision as if she were being held down in a drowning pool. Giving it everything she had, she pushed against it, trying to hold onto this world with spider web hands. The harder she struggled to break free, the heavier the weight became until she succumbed completely, slipping from one reality into another.

She sat at a table in a coffee shop. Across from her, Graham drummed his fingers, striking the tabletop like piano keys. His jaw was clean-shaven, his hair short. Threads of gray were just beginning at his temples.

Beneath the table, his leg pumped as his gaze held hers. No. He looked through her. She turned to see what he stared at so intently.

The door opened and she saw herself walk through it. Graham shot to his feet and waved her over. Realizing she sat in the only other seat at the table, Erin stood just as her future self sat. She shivered at the imagined contact and backed away from the scene. Pressing her eyes closed, she redoubled her efforts to break free of the vision. More pain. She stumbled back, passing through a table where another couple sat, and caught herself before she slipped through the wall and out into the street.

Graham reached for her hand across the table, the one with an engagement ring. She was engaged? To whom? Erin found herself moving closer, unable to pull her gaze from the ring and from Graham as he bent to kiss the back of her hand. It was difficult to read the other Erin's expression. She appeared angry, yet at the same time she seemed to pity Graham as he held her hand in both of his. Erin could see the struggle on her own face. Graham was speaking in earnest and the other Erin was trying hard not to be swayed.

He apologized. *Again.* The word echoed through her mind as if she'd heard all of his apologies on the subject before. Yet how could she? She inched closer, cautious, as though she'd be caught by her future self.

"How many times do you expect me to go through this?" the other Erin asked. "I just want a number so I can know when it will finally stop."

"I didn't ask for any of this," Graham said.

"Neither did I."

"I know I've hurt you—"

"You've gotten very good at it."

"I'm trying. I really am."

"And while you try I'm supposed to do what? Wait around for a fiancé who may or may not come home? Where do you go? What do you do?"

"I..." Graham pulled away, his hands fisting on his thighs under the table.

"You know what? I don't care." Future Erin started to rise.

"Wait! Don't go, Erin. Please."

"Give me a reason not to."

He hesitated and it must have been too much for her. Her voice turned hard. "You're so used to being the one who leaves you don't know what it's like to be left. Do you?" she asked.

"I don't want to hurt you anymore."

"Just go ahead and say it, Graham. I already know. You go to her grave."

Shock, guilt, and relief sifted through Graham's expression like hourglass sand until it ran out and he went blank again.

"You didn't think I'd look?" Future Erin asked. "Didn't think I'd use my ability to find you?"

"You know how I feel about you doing that."

"What else am I supposed to do? Sit around and imagine you dead somewhere?"

"I'm sorry."

"God. If I hear you say that one more time—"

Graham rubbed his thighs with the flat of his hands. "I want to come home."

Other Erin glanced away, close to tears. She sucked in a shuddering breath and let it out slowly.

Graham reached out and stroked her face. "Don't cry, Babe. Please."

Seeing herself suffering snapped something inside Erin and she felt herself being drawn down. Just as the window on her vision closed she heard her future self say, tears in her voice, "You're the only one keeping you away, Graham. And you're the only one who can bring you back to me."

The darkness was total and complete. In the distance Erin heard voices. She could feel a cold hardness beneath her. And then the curtain went up on another scene. She was in Keith's house, standing at the railing of the second floor overlooking his living room. Alone. She'd been in Keith's house just once before and then only briefly. The living room below was as she remembered it, clean and tidy. A place for everything and everything in its place.

It suddenly struck her how odd it was that Keith and Deidre had an affair. Keith was a man who liked neat even rows. It was equally strange that Keith had gone out with someone as messy and unpredictable as Erin. She obviously hadn't known Keith as well as she thought, to be so wrong about the choices he'd made. She wondered where she'd be right now if Deidre, Greg, and Keith hadn't died. Where they'd all be if she could go back to that day on Amiable Lane and alter events.

Keith walked into the room and looked up at the ceiling. He wore the black dress pants and white shirt of his work uniform. His hair was combed, his face freshly shaved. The scent of his cologne wafted up to Erin, bringing with it memories of their time together and the sharp pain of regret. He hadn't been a bad guy. He'd always been respectful and kind toward her. She couldn't help but feel that she'd let him down and had repaid his kindness with reserve instead of interest.

He left the room again, then reappeared with rope and began to climb the stairs. *Oh, no.* She didn't want to see this. She pushed hard against the wall that had sprung up between herself and reality, mentally beating at it, looking for a break she could exploit and escape through. But the wall was pain and the more she worked at it, the stronger it became until she doubled over, nauseous and nearly blinded.

Keith hit the landing and paused. His eyes swam with despair. He looked down at the rope in his hands, then up at the beams in the ceiling, his fingers worrying the rope like a rosary. He was mumbling something, but Erin's ears rang with misery and she couldn't make out the words. He jolted, quaking like an addict denied his fix.

His motions became frantic as he threw the end of the rope at the beam over and over, whipping at it until the end finally sailed over the other side. He jogged downstairs and retrieved the end, then came back up and repeated the process. Three times he wrapped the beam before tying it off. He stared at the other end of the rope as if he didn't know what he was supposed to do with it and then he began to fashion the noose. His movements were jerky and unsure. He paused several times and closed his eyes, shaking as though he was waging an internal war.

Erin redoubled her efforts to break out of the vision, turning away from Keith's trembling form hunched over the knot he was making. She felt the cold hardness again, pressing against her right side. Graham's voice distant and flickering called to her from another time. A fissure formed in the vision, melting one world into the next. Behind her, a loud knock sounded at Keith's front door.

"Keith! Open up. Sherriff." Graham's voice.

Keith began to sob.

In front of her, Erin could see the long expanse of her entryway floor, stretching out into the living room. Graham leaned down into her line of vision. She blinked up at him. At her back, Keith got to his feet. She turned in the vision and the two images overlapped. Graham over Keith. Keith slipped the noose over his head. Graham touched her face. She fought for breath. Fought to move. Keith threw one leg over the railing, then the other.

She reached out for Keith and hit Graham. "No! Don't!"

"Don't what?" Graham asked.

Keith gripped the sides of his head, wincing as though he felt the same pain she did. And then he jumped. She screamed. Graham shook her. Keith kicked, losing a shoe. A lamp crashed. He jerked. The rope squeaked, protesting against the weight.

A pounding on Keith's door. "Sheriff. Open the door!" The doorknob jiggled.

"Keith!" Erin shrieked.

"Erin! Stop it!" Graham gripped her shoulders harder, jostling her against the floor. "It's not real. Snap out of it."

Her head knocked against the hardwood, cracking the pain open. Suddenly she was free of the vision. Thrust back into the here and now. She closed her eyes, then opened them again.

"Graham?"

"Yes." He released her shoulders and smoothed her hair back from her face. "I'm here, Babe."

"I couldn't stop it."

"I tried to reach you."

"I heard you calling."

"You did?" He sagged down onto the floor next to her, laid his head against the cool wood floor. "You scared the crap out of me. What the hell happened?"

She wanted to move, but couldn't find the strength. "I got sucked into one vision and then another. Couldn't break free." She pulled in a shaky breath. "It's never been like that." She put a hand to her head where the pain had nearly split her head in two.

He moved closer. "Are you hurt?"

"I'm okay." But she wasn't. Keith's anguished moan as he'd leapt to his death looped through her head. She rolled onto her back slowly and stared up at the ceiling.

Something wasn't right. She tried to reconcile the Keith in her vision with the Keith she'd known. His expressions and movements didn't match, like a movie out of sync he'd been confusing to watch, his body moving one way while his mind seemed to move in another. What did a person think of when he took his own life? Was he scared? Happy? Relieved?

"You saw Keith in your vision," Graham prompted.

She continued to stare at the ceiling. Graham was hard to look at, knowing how much pain he was going to cause her. But there would be joy, too, she imagined or else why would they move in together? Why would they get engaged? What would make him pull away from her eventually and whose grave would he go to when he'd leave her? This was why she tried hard not to ever look at the future. Why seeing Greg's death had disturbed her so much. She'd not tempted fate by summoning up the future since she was a child and saw the night her mother would leave forever.

"Yes, I did. You were there." She bolted upright, the realization striking with shocking force. "You could've stopped him."

Graham sat up next to her. "Stopped him from what?"

"Oh, my God. You were there. At Keith's house. You were knocking on the front door as he jumped off the balcony."

"Jesus. You saw Keith's death?"

"Didn't you hear him?" She looked off into the distance, trying to remember the details. "You knocked. His shoe fell off and hit the lamp. It crashed to the floor. You banged on the door again and tried to open it." She turned to him. "You might've saved him."

Graham met her gaze and in his eyes she saw realization dawn. "Holy shit. I heard a noise. I just thought he was hiding to keep from answering my questions." He pounded the floor with a fist. "Damn it. I tried to get in, but all the doors were locked. Damn it!"

"I don't think he really wanted to kill himself." His struggle, the jerkiness of his movement. How out of sync his actions were with who he was as a person and the emotions that had played across his face. She really didn't think that Keith wanted to kill himself. He'd fought against it.

"What do you mean?"

"I think someone or something drove him to do it."

"Drove him? Like a mind control kind of thing?"

"Yes. Exactly like mind control."

GRAHAM LEANED BACK against the sofa. The fright of seeing Erin lying unconscious on the floor was just now wearing off, but his heart hadn't gotten the memo. It still pounded out a fight-or-flight beat. He pulled in a deep breath and let it out slowly. This day had been a shit-fest from the moment he'd stepped out onto Erin's porch that morning. And now she was trying to tell him that there might be someone in San Rey with the ability to control other people's thoughts. Fucking hell.

"How is that possible?" he asked.

"Oh, my God!" She popped up to her feet and began to pace. "Greg."

He followed suit, moving slower than she had. "You think someone got to Greg too?"

"I know it sounds crazy. It *is* crazy. Let me try and

explain—" She suddenly clamped both hands to the side of her head and squeezed her eyes shut, swaying.

"Erin!" He raced to her side and put his hands over hers. "Erin. Make it stop. Come on, Babe. You can do it."

She sucked in air and her eyes popped open. "I was just thinking about Greg and the pain hit. I started to see him and then you pulled me back. What the hell is going on?'

The fear in her voice shook him. He wouldn't let her see how much. "Just hang on to me." He pulled her hands down and held them in his. "I'm right here."

"Someone is doing this. Someone with a powerful ability."

"How?"

"I don't know. But he knows about me, knows how to bend my ability and turn it against me." She put a hand on his chest and gripped his shirt, bringing him closer. "He's doing the same thing to my dad and my aunt."

He could see she believed what she was saying. How could this be? A person with an undiscovered ability, running around San Rey, using his influence to make people kill themselves? How was that possible? He couldn't wrap his head around it. And then he thought of the interviews he'd done over the past few weeks. Over and over people told him how they didn't know why they'd done the things he was arresting them for. The thought had struck them and they'd felt compelled to act on it. As though they had no choice. No free will.

"I think he compelled Greg and Keith to take their own lives," Erin was saying, her voice full of purpose and determination. "He probably killed Deidre. In fact, I know he did. I think that's what started this whole thing. He killed Deidre and is using his ability to distract you and the entire town from what he's done."

"Compelled. That's an interesting word." And consistent with what had been happening. Turning it around in his head, he could see it. The person manipulating people into committing crimes and worse, had to be in possession of a very strong ability. Erin had shied away from the word power, but in this instance, it fit.

"He targeted my aunt because she can read minds and my dad because he can put suggestions into people's heads," Erin continued. "I can see the past and future. I've actually *seen* what he's done. He's twisting our abilities, using them against us."

He couldn't deny what she was saying. At the same time he didn't want to believe it. A murderer with the ability to command others to do terrible things. Things they would never do on their own. If what Erin was saying was true, there was a serial killer in San Rey(?).

6

"You don't believe me," Erin said.

Graham let out a frustrated breath. "It's not that."

"Then what is it?"

Graham rubbed her shoulder. They sat side by side on the couch in front of the fire. Outside the wind had kicked up, rushing through the trees and rattling the windows. Inside the fire leapt and spat, licking up in spiraling tendrils. Every once in a while, the wind dashed down the chimney and flattened it, but the fire would surge up again, more determined than ever to burn on. A lot like Erin and her indomitable spirit, he thought.

"How do we find out who it is and stop them?" he asked. "Is there some kind of ability detector? Can you or your aunt or your dad tell if someone you meet has a talent of some kind?"

"It doesn't work like that."

"Have you ever met anyone else with abilities?"

She shook her head.

He waited a beat then asked, "Did your mother have an ability?"

"No." Her answer closed the door on any other questions he might have had about that side of her family.

He leaned his head back against the couch and closed his eyes. He still shook inside from seeing Erin lying on the floor, her gaze fixed and blank. He'd thought for a moment that she was dead and it was Patricia all over again without all the blood and the sickening knowledge that he was to blame. Only it *would* be his fault if something happened to Erin.

He sat up and turned to face her. "I have to tell you something." He hadn't meant to blurt it out, but if he couldn't be honest with himself, he could at least be honest with her.

She shifted, pulling away from him a little. "What."

Not a question. Maybe she already knew. That was why she'd been acting suspicious toward him, standoff-ish. Even now he could feel her withdrawing from him, watching him as though he'd turn on her at any moment. She deserved better than him, better than a son who couldn't stand up to his father, better than the failure he was. She was right to mistrust him. He would let her down as he'd let Patricia down. He was a disappointment to his father, this town, himself.

"What, Graham?"

He looked down at her hand on his arm, then up into her eyes. The wariness was there, but at the center was something he hadn't expected and didn't deserve.

She cared for him. He'd have to find a way to nurture it, make it crowd out the doubt until it disappeared entirely.

"I came here to break things off between us."

Her head jolted back a little and her lips parted. She hadn't been expecting him to say that. Then what—

"Why?" she was asking, her hands now clenched in her lap. "I mean okay. Sure. If that's what you want."

"No, I—"

She took a breath and lifted her chin. "It was a stupid idea anyway and never would have worked out. You're right. It's best to end things now. I guess I should thank you."

"Is that what *you* want?"

"It doesn't seem to—" Her body went stiff and she clamped her eyes shut, grabbing her head in her hands. "The...pain."

He dropped to his knees in front of her and gripped her forearms. "Erin. Break out of it." He gave her a little shake. "Stop it!"

Her eyes popped open. She blinked slowly as though she expected the pain to strike again.

"Gone?"

"Yeah. I think so. You can let go of me."

He eased back, his heart pounding so hard, the backs of his eyes stung. "It hit faster that time."

"I'm fine now. You can go."

"What if I don't want to?"

"I'm not up for any more of your games."

"What do you mean any more?"

She pressed her lips together and shook her head as though breaking free from thoughts she couldn't trace. "Nothing. Poor choice of words."

"Let me start again." He returned to the sofa, giving her the space she seemed to want. "I came here *intending* to break up with you."

"Yeah, we went over that part."

"But I don't want to."

"Graham, I'm tired. This has been a really, *really* crappy day." She rose and moved to the door. "I think you should leave."

He jumped up and followed her, the need to make her understand riding him hard. He was going to disappoint someone either way. It may as well be the person who was used to it. "Let me explain."

Sighing, she leaned back against the front door and crossed her arms over her chest. He would only get one shot at this.

"I'm an idiot, I know."

"You're finally starting to make some sense."

He couldn't help the smile that tugged at the corner of his lips. God, he loved her smart mouth. "I couldn't do it. I don't want this to stop. Whatever is going on between us is good. Well, I think it's good."

She gave a reluctant nod, spurring him on.

"My pop thinks you're a...distraction."

"He knows about us?"

"Yeah."

"And he doesn't approve," she said, her tone as defensive as the look on her face.

"I didn't say that."

"You really are an idiot."

"He's sick. He's not seeing things clearly."

"I know what your father thinks of my family. I've grown up with that attitude my whole life. I get it. He doesn't want his precious son contaminated by the likes of me."

"You're wrong." But she wasn't. That was exactly what his father had said.

"We're done here." She started to pull the door open, but he slammed it closed hard enough to rattle the windows and send her staggering.

He gripped her shoulders, steadying her. "We're not done."

"Don't you get it? We were finished before we started. It was stupid to think this could work."

"What about last night?"

Something aching and hot flashed in her eyes and she swallowed hard. He could almost hear her heart pounding in her chest, could see the pulse throbbing in her neck. He breathed in her scent and before he thought to do it, he was tracing a finger from her jaw to the hollow of her clavicle and back again. She shuddered. He eased closer and replaced his finger with his mouth, licking kisses under her jaw to her ear. She put her hands on his shoulders, but didn't push him away. Instead she held him there, their bodies brushing but not touching.

"What about last night?" he asked again, whispering the question over her skin, causing dots of her flesh to rise as though she were chilled. "What about tonight?"

"We shouldn't."

"Please let me stay."

Her fingers flexed on his shoulders, kneading. He leaned in, pressing his body against hers. She could probably feel his erection, but that wasn't why he wanted to stay.

"Let me care for you," he found himself saying, the headiness of being near her heavy in his voice. "Just that. Nothing else. Please."

"Okay. Yes."

Her words washed through him. He might not have heard her if she hadn't had her face buried in the side of his neck. But it wasn't satisfaction that flooded his system. It was relief. He'd nearly blown it with her, still might yet. But for now she accepted him, maybe even wanted him. He'd take that. He'd take whatever she was willing to give. He knew then that he could take anything—his father's disappointment, failure in front of the town, anything—as long as she stood with him.

Wrapping his arms around her, he nearly groaned at the feel of her body lined up against his. There was no way to deny what was between them. No way to hide from it. His father would just have to understand...or not. Most likely not.

As they turned to head to her bedroom, Erin wondered how he'd done it. Somehow he always managed to change her mind at the last moment. Or maybe she'd wanted her mind changed. She really hadn't wanted him to leave. He'd started to talk about breaking up and her self-preservation instincts had kicked in. And the next thing she knew, she was asking him to leave, practically throwing him out. When he'd slammed the door shut and asked to stay, she'd been so relieved.

They went into the bedroom and through the motions of getting ready for bed. He used the extra toothbrush she'd given him the night before. It still sat in the holder next to hers. It looked right there. As did his reflection beside hers in the mirror. They slipped into bed and she turned to him, expecting they'd make love. Instead he brought her close and held her, tucking her tightly to him. She smoothed her cheek on his chest, luxuriating in the feel of his skin against hers. His scent was familiar now and she craved it.

They would stay together long enough to fall in love, move in together, get engaged...hurt each other. This was why she hated looking at the future. Premonition never brought her anything but heartache. And too many unanswerable questions.

Light flashed behind her eyes, bright and white hot. Her head felt as though it would crumble under the incredible pressure. Graham's scent lingered, like a blown out candle, flittering at the edges of her consciousness. She could almost hear the echo of him calling her from far away.

She stood at the edge of a pool of blood. In the center of it lay the woman with dark hair and sightless eyes from her earlier vision. Across the room, Graham bent nearly in two, gripping his bleeding side and gagging back vomit. The fat man Graham had argued with sat on the floor, his head on his chest. A trail of blood smeared down the wall behind him.

Erin started to shake. Graham shouted her name, the sound reverberated inside of her, bouncing away and back so she couldn't grasp it to know if it was real. The Graham in her vision stumbled over to the woman and dropped to his knees beside her. His face twisted with grief. He mumbled something, took a deep breath, and began to search the woman's body. Finding nothing, he stopped. Gripping his knees, he sucked in a shaky breath. His gaze shifted to her torso.

"Goddammit, Patricia," he murmured. And then he pulled her shirt up, exposing her bra. He reached toward her, then pulled his hand away. "Goddammit." As though mentally preparing himself, Graham inhaled deeply, squaring his shoulders. Then he pulled her bra up, exposing her breasts and a small, black cylinder taped between them with a thin wire attached to it. Graham pried it loose and rolled her to trace the wire. He removed a small black recorder-looking thing that was taped to the small of her back.

From far away, Graham's voice grew insistent, but Erin ignored it, fascinated by the scene before her of this other Graham, stuffing the recorder into his pocket, then putting the woman's clothing back to rights.

"I'm sorry," he whispered, stroking her cheek with the backs of his fingers.

A show of affection that Erin had thought belonged only to her. It wasn't clear what this woman—Patricia —was to Graham, but it was clear they'd been lovers, had maybe even been in love. Whatever they'd been, it was something less than that now. The regret etched into Graham's features, the same expression he'd shown Erin in the future, recounted a litany of failings and failure, of inescapable culpability and conflict.

He stood and looked around. Sirens pealed in the distance, spurring Graham into action. He pulled a gun from the back of his waistband and used the hem of his shirt to wipe it down. Careful not to touch it, he bent over, wincing in pain, and put it in Patricia's hand, pressing her fingers to the trigger and the grip. He stood and rubbed his hands on his pants, gave the room one last look, then left, taking care not to touch the knob on his way out.

Erin knelt beside Patricia and put her hand to the woman's forehead. Suddenly she was shoved back out of this room full of death and into another, sun filled room. Curtains fluttered in the hot afternoon breeze. Outside, the city went about its day, sending up street noise as evidence. Erin went to the window and gazed out, trying to get her bearings. She didn't recognize the room or the view. Los Angeles maybe? She glanced around and spied a group of photos on an end table.

Making her way over to them, she noticed the feminine touches in the room— a ruffled pillow, a black and white print of a flower, a pair of high heels on the floor, and the photo frames. Only a woman would choose something so ornate and delicate. Patricia's lovely face gazed back at Erin, her smile wide and infectious. She stood next to a woman who looked remarkably like her. A sister, perhaps. The next photo made Erin gasp, her hand flying to her mouth. Graham and Patricia locked in an embrace, clearly more than friends.

Erin's gaze swung to the next photo of Patricia and Graham again. This time they were both in uniform—dress blues—standing side by side. The familiarity in this photo was suppressed, but there if you knew to look for it. Patricia had been an L.A.P.D. cop just like Graham. Had they worked together? What had happened between them, leading up to the scene in that cheap apartment?

A laugh down the hall brought Erin's attention back to her surroundings. She started to look around for a place to hide before she remembered that she couldn't be seen by whoever was coming into the room. This wasn't real. None of this was real. The past. Nothing but the past.

Patricia came into the room; her laugh, full and bright, entered ahead of her. She glanced back at someone following her. "You hate Branson. And he hates you. I don't know why you'd want to go."

Graham appeared behind Patricia and Erin stumbled back a step. He looked like the old Graham, the one who stared back at her from the pages of her high school yearbook. So young. So unencumbered.

He snagged Patricia around the waist and brought her up against him. "Maybe I just want to be where you are." He nuzzled her neck, blatantly running a hand up to her breast.

Erin's chest burned, watching them together. Her internal chant of *this is not real, this is the past* was abruptly cut off as Patricia moaned and gripped

Graham's ass, grinding her pelvis against his. Erin clamped her hands over her ears and squeezed her eyes closed tight, but not before she saw Graham kiss Patricia, pressing his lips to hers as he wrestled with the buttons on her blouse.

The room was suddenly hot, stifling. Then Graham's lips were on hers, his body against hers, as he'd been with Patricia. Erin opened her eyes and saw Graham nose to nose with her. He yelled something and then pressed his mouth to hers again. Through him she could see the other Graham—the past Graham—leading Patricia back to the bedroom as he shucked his shirt and Patricia laughed.

Erin closed her eyes and focused all her energy into what she knew to be real—the feel of Graham's lips on hers, his body covering hers. And slowly the sounds from the other bedroom faded away, replaced by the sound of Graham's rough breathing as he broke the kiss. She opened her eyes again to find him hovering over her, his face creased with concern.

"Finally," he said, collapsing against her. He held her tight, mashing her arms to her sides and whooshing the breath out of her. Just as suddenly he released her, searching her face once again, making sure she was really in the here and now. "Say something." He smoothed the hair back from her brow. "Erin..."

"I'm here. I'm...back."

He crushed her to him again, this time not as hard. "Thank God. I didn't know what to do. I was about to call for an ambulance."

"How long...?"

He released her. "Twenty minutes, half an hour. I don't know. I tried everything I could think of to get you back."

"Kissing? What am I? Sleeping Beauty?"

"You can joke when I'm nearly hoarse from yelling your name?"

She sat up and realized her nightgown and the bed around her was damp. "Why am I wet?"

"Cold water. Ice. Warm water. I tried it all."

"And only the kiss worked?"

"I was desperate." He adjusted his position, sitting across from her. "Where did you go?"

He asked the question as though she'd made the choice to leave. As though she'd left him on purpose when it was him who would leave her. She wanted to get defensive with him, blame him for all she'd seen as though he'd only just done it. But she was the only one at fault here. She'd purposefully focused on Patricia, drawing herself into that last scene. She had wanted to know more about the woman and the events that would haunt Graham from within like some parasitic specter.

What had happened between him and Patricia that had led to the events in that apartment and her death? Graham still carried the guilt over it, would carry it for years, dragging it into his and Erin's future lives together. She wanted to ask him about it, grill him for every detail, but she'd made a promise to her father a long time ago that she wouldn't ever talk about what she saw in her visions. Talking about someone's past with them before they could tell it themselves would change the natural course of things and might somehow alter the future.

The future. The future was a monster she could confront but never vanquish. She hated it. Hated the knowing and yet not knowing enough. And now he wanted to know what she couldn't tell him.

So instead she looked him square in the eye and lied. "I went back to when I was a child."

"Uh huh."

He didn't believe her. She pulled her knees up to her chest and hugged her legs, rocking a little. She'd have to give him something here. Maybe if she did, he'd give her something in return. "My mom..." She cleared her throat and started again, but the lump in her throat stuck. "My mom left when I was eight. I'd had a vision about it a week before. I told my dad about it. I wanted him to stop her, to do something to keep her from leaving us."

"But he didn't."

She shook her head. "He got mad at me for telling him. He told me that he wouldn't be stopping her from leaving. I think I told him I hated him. I don't know." She looked away, hiding sudden tears. She hated that she still cried over a woman who never gave her a backwards thought. "He forbade me from looking at the future ever again and he said that if I told my mom what I'd seen that she'd probably only leave sooner. So I kept my mouth shut and got an extra week with her because of it." Her voice broke as the tears spilled over.

Graham reached for her, but she pulled away. She

didn't want his pity. She wanted his truth. Swiping at her eyes, she continued. "I never looked at the future again until the day my boss handed me the Lasiter file and I accidentally saw Greg dead."

"I'm sorry."

"It was a long time ago."

"No. I'm sorry that you'd rather dig up an old, painful memory than tell me the truth."

7

E rin looked at him with haunted eyes. Graham was sorry about that, too. Sorry she didn't trust him enough to tell him the truth. She'd offered up that story about her mother too easily. What could she possibly have seen...?

Oh, shit. *Patricia.* He could see it on her now, the questions piling up behind her beautiful eyes. She didn't want to ask. She *wouldn't* ask. She'd divulged that story about her mother to get him to confide in her about Patricia. How much had she seen? How far back had she gone? What did she know? How in the hell could he tell her any of it when he couldn't bear to look at it himself?

She'd tried to trade a part of herself for a part of him, an ugly memory for an ugly memory. Except his past transgressions ran colder and more dangerous than childhood heartbreak. He'd betrayed someone who'd trusted him, someone he loved and who had loved him in return. How could he possibly explain the reasons why, when he hadn't fully accepted them himself?

She was already looking at him differently. The worry and fear he'd felt for her during her episode boiled over. His breath came harsher, his heart thundered in his chest. The edges of his vision hazed red and still she sat there, silently pleading with him to tell her everything. She'd gone behind his back and riffled through his past, looking for what?

"And what is the truth, Graham?" Her appeal was small and sad, lacking reproach.

"What do you want from me?"

She didn't flinch at his anger. She just sat there, watching, waiting. The light from the bedside lamp cast half her face in shadow, but he didn't need to see her full expression to feel her disappointment. It wrapped around him, lashing him to her like a prisoner.

"What do you *want*?" he asked again, his voice betraying his inner turmoil.

"I'm sorry. I..." She scrubbed her hands over her face. "I should know better. I'm sorry."

He pretended he didn't see the tears she tried to hide, but they took a nick out of him, marring his already damaged soul. He gulped back the rising pain. He'd hurt her. Again. Maybe his father was right. Maybe they *were* wrong for each other, but he'd gotten the most important part wrong. Erin wasn't the one lacking, Graham was.

"I shouldn't have done it," she was saying. "I knew better, but I couldn't help it. I'm not like my aunt. Or I wasn't. I don't try to look into people's lives, prying where I don't belong. That's not me."

So she had seen something about him, something she'd purposefully set out to find.

"I want you to know," she continued, "that I didn't get to choose where the—"

She pressed the heels of her hands into the sides of her head and squeezed her eyes shut, taking slow, deep breaths. He started toward her, but she waved him off.

"I've got this. Give me..." More deep breaths. "...a minute." After a few moments more, she sighed heavily and opened her eyes. "Okay. It's gone." Her sudden smile twisted his gut. "I did it. I did it all by myself."

He couldn't help the half smile he gave her in return. "Good job."

"Thanks." She grew serious again, twisting the edge of her nightgown. "This thing, this whatever it is that's happening to me, it's changed my ability. I used to be able to choose when and who I saw. Now, it's like if I think about someone, *bam*, I'm there, past or present. I thought about Keith and saw his death with no decision on my part. None at all."

The fist-sized knot in his chest loosened. Whatever she'd seen of his past wasn't her choice then. She hadn't gone behind his back.

"At least at first," she said.

"What do you mean *at first*?"

"This last time I went from vision to vision. The first one I didn't choose, but the second one... I purposefully changed the vision. I was wrong to do it and I'm sorry."

The knot was back. "Changed how?"

"I can't tell you. If I tell you it could alter the future."

"Between us."

"Yes."

"What am I supposed to say? You went into my past... I'm assuming my past?" She nodded, confirming his worst fears. "On purpose. Looking for what?"

"I don't know."

"You don't... Jesus."

"I'm sorry."

"Yeah, well that helps." He rose from the bed and began to pace, trying to smother the clawing panic. "Do I get to rummage through your drawers now? Go through your things? Know things about you that aren't any of my goddamned business?"

"I'm sorry."

"I got that."

"I shouldn't have done it."

"No shit."

"There's no way to make it up to you, I know."

"And I don't even get to know what part of my life's been violated?"

"I can't."

He stopped and stared at her, the nightmare growing, spreading like a cancer against her. "*You can't* is awfully convenient."

"That's not fair."

Un-fucking-believable. "Fair?" He stalked toward the bed. To her credit, she didn't flinch or shrink away. "You want fair?" he demanded. "What would be fair here, Erin, is you telling me what the hell is going on. You can tell me all about your visions of the killer and of

Keith, but when you pry into my past, all of a sudden you play the *I Can't Change the Future* card. Bullshit."

"That's not the same."

"Isn't it? Your visions have already changed the future. If you hadn't shared what you'd seen about the killer I would've accepted the D.A.'s decision that Greg and Deidre's deaths were exactly as they appeared— murder/suicide. I wouldn't have considered Keith a suspect until you told me about your visions. And maybe he wouldn't have killed himself if you hadn't confronted him about your vision of him and Deidre."

Her hands flew to her mouth and she sucked in a breath. That was a cheap shot on his part, but the anger and fear made him not care. She'd done this to him, to them.

"Which is it, Erin? Because you can't have it both ways."

"You're a bastard."

"Maybe so, but at least I'm honest."

"Yeah, you're *so* honest." She came up to her knees on the bed, her gaze nearly level with his. "You're so honest you killed that man and put the gun in Patricia's hand. You're so honest you wiped everything down so no one would know you were even in that apartment. So *honest* that you left her there alone, dead. You loved her and just left her."

"That's it. Go on. Don't stop now. What else did you see?"

"I saw you pull up her shirt, her bra, and remove a recording device."

"What else?"

"I saw you kissing her, touching her."

"Touching her how?"

"Don't make me say it."

"Is that the part you had to see?" he asked, his voice punishing. "Me *fucking* her?"

"Stop it!"

"You wanted to know about her. You had to look. Don't chicken out now. Ask me about it. Cast your judgment."

"Oh, God. Is that what you want?"

"It's too late to ask me what I want. This is all about what you want."

HE WANTED her to reject him, he expected it, Erin realized. He stood there defiant and noble, ready to accept his punishment. Whatever penance he'd dealt himself wasn't enough. He'd judged himself harshly and had come up lacking. He watched her with eyes full of despair. And suddenly she saw what she'd been missing.

He'd been right. She had manipulated the future by confiding in Graham about her visions. And her visions of Graham's life were nothing more than scenes taken out of context. What had happened before and between mattered more than what she'd seen. She needed the whole picture. They both did.

She sank back down on the bed and patted the spot next to her. "Come, sit."

He eyed her as though it was some kind of trick.

"Please."

He sat, but not next to her, choosing instead the end of the bed and the furthest he could get away from her and still comply. That was something, she guessed.

"How did you and Patricia meet?"

"God. Why do you want to know about this? What's the point?"

"It's time we laid everything out because the past isn't all I've seen. I've also seen the future. This doesn't go away for you, for us. I care about you, Graham. And I think you care about me."

She took his no-answer as confirmation.

"You were on the L.A.P.D. together," she began. "Is that how you met?"

"Why don't we start with what you don't already know?"

She'd have to pull it from him an inch at a time. Fine. "Were you partners?"

"No. Not at first."

GRAHAM COULD STILL REMEMBER the first time he'd seen Patricia. Her long, dark hair had been tied back and tucked under her dress uniform cap. She'd taken the loss of her partner stoically, her back rigid as his casket was lowered into the ground. He couldn't help but stare at her. She'd caught him looking and when their gazes had connected he'd felt like he'd been punched in the gut. All of the air whooshed out of him. From that moment, he'd made a point of putting himself in her path.

"Were you dating before you became partners?"

Erin asked, breaking into long suppressed memories best forgotten.

"No. After."

"Isn't there some kind of rule against partners dating?"

"That rule didn't apply to Patricia and me."

"Why not?"

"I was under orders."

"You were ordered to have an affair with your partner?"

"Yes. Sort of. No, not really. It just sort of happened and they wanted to use it. I let them."

She shook her head, trying to follow what he was saying. "Your superiors?"

"No. Internal Affairs."

"They thought Patricia was a dirty cop?"

"What makes you think it was her and not me?"

"Because I know you."

He snorted and looked away. "Yeah, well..." She didn't know him as well as she thought.

"Was she dirty?"

"I didn't believe it at first. I agreed to what they wanted, thinking I could get her cleared. They suspected she was involved in her partner's death. It was all a mistake. It had to be. She wouldn't do what they were accusing her of. By the time I realized that it was much worse than they'd thought, we were..."

"In love?"

He shook his head. "I don't know what we were." And that was the truth. What they might have been had been stunted from the start. He'd poisoned the ground so that nothing could grow between them.

"You cared about her. I can see it."

"Maybe." Yes. God, yes.

"Did she know you were working for Internal Affairs?"

He nodded.

"You told her, didn't you?"

He'd never forget the look on Patricia's face when he'd confronted her, when he had to tell her that they'd been a lie. That he'd been using her, fucking her, to get what he could for IAB. She'd slapped him. Screamed at him. He just stood there and took it all. His original motives didn't matter anymore. He deserved everything she threw at him and more. While she'd been talking about a future together, marriage, he'd been collecting evidence against her. Every single day they were together.

"I tried to help her, tried to get her out of it. Tried to convince her we could have a life together. That deal in the apartment was supposed to have been the last of it. She promised. But I had a feeling she was up to something. It all went down too easily...at first."

"She shot you."

He self-consciously rubbed his side where the bullet had hit. That had been the biggest surprise of all. If he hadn't had seen Franklin's reaction to Patricia pulling her gun in that last split second before she fired, he might not be here right now, calmly discussing the whole fucking mess with Erin.

"Yeah."

"The other guy shot her."

"Franklin. I think he thought she was shooting at him."

"And then you shot Franklin and made it look like Patricia and Franklin had shot each other."

"He would've shot me if I hadn't beaten him to it. It's my fault she's dead. I pushed her into that deal, pushed her to get out. She didn't want to do it. But I promised her... Ah, shit." He got up from the bed and moved to the window. He couldn't look at Erin when he told this next part. He hooked a finger in the curtain and pulled it aside. The night was still and solemn. A cruel contrast to the blackness that roiled inside him.

"I told her I'd tank the IAB case," he said, his breath fogging the window and obscuring the view. "I told her I thought we should get married."

"Why?"

"Spouses can't testify against spouses."

Erin could hardly believe it. The blow of how much Patricia must have meant to Graham hit her hard. It was stupid to be jealous of a dead woman, but the burning ache had settled in her chest and no amount self-chastisement could loosen it. "You would've married her to save her? You loved her that much?"

Graham turned from the window. "I owed her that much."

"So it was obligation, then?"

"Does it matter what it was?"

"I suppose it shouldn't. Why did she have that recorder on her?"

"I found out later she'd gone behind my back and tried to make a deal. She'd offered me up, said I'd been in on it with her from the start, that I'd been playing IAB. It might've worked if she hadn't died. If I hadn't found that recorder and the other evidence she'd manufactured against me."

"Is that why you left L.A.?"

"My dad's heart attack gave me a good reason."

"Did you go to her funeral?"

"Yeah."

Erin could see now how much what he'd gone through had stripped from him. He stood by the window, swallowed in grief, obligation and blame. So much blame. As though he were solely responsible for the choices Patricia had made. Her death hung from him, a weighty sacrifice in the war he waged with his conscience. She couldn't relieve him of it, but maybe she could help him forget, at least for a little while.

And maybe she had some things to forget too.

She rose from the bed and went to him, her damp nightgown sticking to her. He watched her, his body stiff and unmoving.

She slid her hand in his and gave it a little tug. "Come back to bed. It's late."

Cocking his head to the side, he frowned as though he didn't quite understand what she was saying.

She pulled on his hand again. "Come on."

He allowed her to tow him back to the bed and climbed in next to her. She peeled off her wet nightgown and threw it on the floor. He continued to watch her, his gaze hot and wary. She placed a hand on his chest and leaned in to kiss him.

He pulled away. "What are you doing?"

"I thought that was fairly obvious."

"Why?"

"I want something outside my head, something real and tangible and immediate. I just want to *feel*."

He reached out to brush the backs of his fingers over her cheek. She caught his hand and held it in both of hers against her bare chest.

"Can you understand that?" she asked. "Can you do that for me?"

He stared at her for a moment, his expression giving away the rapid play of his emotions. And then he reached out and gripped the back of her head and brought her down for a kiss. Light and restrained, he tasted, testing. She let him go slow, let him feel his way to her.

Her skin felt feverish and prickly against his. Her senses spiraled into overdrive, the sensations piling up, one on top of the other and still he kissed her as though he had all the time in the world or was committing this moment to memory. *Oh, my God that was it.* She pushed back, breaking the kiss to look down at him. He was ending things. She could feel his withdrawal as though it was a string he pulled, unraveling everything between them.

Reaching down, she grabbed the sheet and drew it around her. She couldn't speak, could only watch and wait while he settled their fate. He leaned up on his elbows. The late hour and all she'd been though tonight must have messed her up more than she thought. That couldn't be a smile. He wasn't the kind of guy to grin while he busted her heart into unrecognizable pieces. Crooked as it was, it was a smile. The self-deprecating, it's-not-you-it's-me kind of smile that locked her lungs.

"Just say it," she dared.

"We're going to do it my way this time."

"What?"

"Slow." He rose up and stalked toward her on hands and knees. "Torturously slow."

She backed away on instinct. "Wha...what will you do?"

He had her against the headboard now. "You wanted mindless." He hooked a finger in the sheet and drew it slowly down. "You wanted to *feel*."

Her lips parted at the look in his eyes. "Yes," she breathed.

"You're going to feel me on you...in you. And just when you think I'm done, that you can't take any more, I'll do it all over again."

"Do it."

A DARE. Graham liked it. He liked her and everything about her. She didn't come with a set of rules he was supposed to follow, a predetermined mold he was supposed to shape himself into. He could just be and she accepted. With her, he was both vulnerable and invincible. There was no agenda between them, no competition in which he had to constantly look over his shoulder, wondering when she'd plunge the knife into his back. He'd told her the worst, expecting judgment. Instead he'd been given acceptance.

And now after all she knew of him, she wanted to take him into her body, to be his at least for tonight. Instead of satisfaction, he found the idea intolerable to the point of pain. One night wouldn't be enough. He'd have to find a way to make her want him again and again until they were both finally sated and he could leave her to find a man worthy of her.

Backing up his boast, he took her mouth, kissing her as he'd love her—long, slow, and so thoroughly, she'd cry out his name in pleasure long after they were over. She met him kiss for kiss, thrusting her hands in his hair and drawing him down on top of her. The feel of her under him, wrapping herself around him, struck something base and primal within him. She was his and not just for the night.

He bit her breast, sucking gently as she gasped and clutched him tighter. He pulled back to see what he'd done. His mark, his brand on her skin. *His.* She squirmed, drawing his attention to where he was seated between her thighs. She shifted again and he had to put a hand on her hip to still her movements.

"Slow," he whispered, bending his head to take her nipple into his mouth.

She arched back, presenting her full breasts to him, as he reached down between her legs. Wet. So wet. For him. He wanted to pull his head back and howl like the beast he was for the things he was about to do to her.

He left her breast to work her panties down her legs, weaving a trail of kisses across her abdomen and down one thigh.

Murmuring a protest, she tried to bring him back up her body, but he liked where he was. From the foot of the bed he saw her as he'd never seen her before. She was a feast laid out just for him. He took her feet in his hands, caressing her arches. She sighed and settled back, watching him with eyes that pierced straight through all of his bullshit.

He wanted to pull her to him right then, open her legs, and drive deep. But he'd promised her slow. Sliding his hands up the back of her calves, he drew light circles with his fingertips on the underside of her knees. She closed her eyes and tilted her head back. He pressed her legs open, breathing in the scent of her, basic and tempting. But he wasn't after the now. He wanted her to remember him, remember this night, and compare all others to it.

Her skin was so soft, so pliant. He raised her knees, exposing her deep center. She'd wanted mindless, to feel nothing but sensation, wantonness, abandon. He'd give her that and more. His mouth was a tool he used to drive her, licking up her thighs, nipping, kissing, until she thrashed about, her pelvis tilting. And still he didn't relent. He kissed her everywhere and yet not where she craved it the most.

By the time he crawled up her body, sweaty with exertion, she begged him to come, begged him to release the tension he'd strung out between them. And when he finally thrust into her, heard her cry out his name, he knew he was lost. He'd never make love to a woman like he'd loved her. Would never feel the completion he felt with her.

As their bodies cooled and their hearts beat a regular rhythm, he knew he'd never feel the way he felt in that moment. Would never again love a woman the way he loved her. *Her.* He sucked in great lungfuls of air, knowing he was lost and not caring a lick about it.

8

The grayed light of daybreak filtered through the curtains, illuminating the bed where they lay entwined. They'd remained tethered all night, never breaking contact, an unspoken need to remain bound. If she moved away, he followed. If he rolled, she rolled with him. And now she lay alone in the bed, listening to the water hit the shower tiles. Graham had told her to stay in bed and get some more sleep, but she'd been unable to without him beside her. She snuggled deeper into the bed, feeling connected to Graham in a way she'd never experienced before.

Their discussion, argument, whatever, had shifted something between them. She understood so much more about him now. And had a feeling he'd shared more with her than he'd wanted to, but in the end, not as much as he needed to. That was okay. She could wait. Loving him wasn't going to be easy, but it would certainly have its rewards. She squirmed, thinking about all the things she'd done with him last night. Dirty, naughty things.

He'd driven her to the edge, then pulled her back over and over to the point where she'd begged him for release. And when he'd finally relented, had finally thrust hard into her, she'd cried out—his name, the lord's, incoherent nonsense—until she'd gone hoarse and her lips went numb. He'd followed shortly after, hitting deep on a long, low groan. They'd lain like that, joined in the most intimate way possible until he'd shifted, lifting some of his weight off her. He'd gazed down at her with the most endearingly quizzical look, as though he couldn't quite fathom what they'd done. All she could do was stare back at him, mirroring his expression. If he didn't have the answer, how could she?

The water shut off and her gaze tracked to the window where the sun was just making its ascent, bringing a new day filled with old problems. A killer was still out there, probably planning his next move. Her father and aunt were still ill and she had only been able to hang on as long as she had because of Graham. The pain hadn't come again since she'd fought it back the night before, but she could feel it hovering, waiting to swoop down and strike.

There had to be a way to make it all stop. A way to find a killer with an ability similar to hers and her family's. But how? There were precious few clues as to his identity. It wasn't like they could put an ad in the paper or stand in the middle of town and ask passersby if they'd committed murder.

But wait.

That's exactly what they could do.

She rubbed her eyes and yawned as Graham came into the room. Everything was lighter now with full morning, but it took her a moment to realize that something had changed. Blinking his face into focus, she couldn't believe what she was seeing.

"What did you do?" she asked, sitting up.

He sat on the edge of the bed, his face set and serious. Taking her hand, he placed it on his jaw. "I shaved."

She wriggled closer and put both hands on his face. "You look so different."

"You don't like it."

"I'm just surprised. It's been a while since I've seen your whole face." And he was even more handsome than she remembered.

"It'll make my pop happy." Resentment bled through words that should've held resignation.

"Is that why you did it?"

"No."

"Good."

Something fierce and determined burned low and bright in the depths of his eyes. No. He hadn't done this for his father. He'd done this for himself and maybe her too. He sat up straighter, his shoulders back, chin high, like a warrior preparing for battle. Warmth spread through her, beginning in her chest and radiating out to every point in her body. Pride maybe...or a deeper kind of recognition that went beyond affection and connection. There wasn't a part of her that didn't seem to know him.

"Come here." She pulled him forward and rubbed her cheek against his. "Mmm, nice." He smelled of soap and toothpaste. She imagined more mornings like this, just the two of them cocooned in their own little world.

He moved back. "Keep that up and I won't be able to leave."

"I wish you wouldn't."

"So do I, but I have a killer to catch."

She leaned back against the headboard, his words causing the world to crash back down in flaming chunks around them. Although things had changed between them, nothing had changed around them.

"Any ideas on how to do that?" she asked.

"A few. Yes." He swelled with new purpose. "I also got a text that some of the lab results are in. So I'll go over those and see if anything pops."

She nodded, knowing as well as he did that those results would yield little information. They were dealing with a murderer who could kill without even being in the same room. The only exception was Deidre's murder. Her murder was the only one in which he was physically present. Maybe they'd get lucky there.

"I have to go." He leaned in and kissed her goodbye.

Although she knew he didn't want to leave, she could feel his job pulling at him. A stray thought of taking a quick peek into the future lit across her synapses, stilling her for a moment. She pushed it away with a shake of her head.

"More pain?" he asked.

"No. Just a weird, random thought."

He grinned, going for light. "Weird and random *would* describe your thought process."

"Gee, thanks. Great morning after game you got there. You really know how to sweet talk the ladies."

"Don't need talk when I've got skills."

"Maybe you should stay here and back up that boast."

"No." He kissed her hard and quick, then rose from the bed and backed toward the door. "Stop tempting me."

"Yeah, bed head and morning breath are oh so tempting."

"On you they are." He glanced back as though someone called to him from the other room. "I really do have to go."

"I know. Be careful."

"You, too. Call me if you need me, okay?"

"Yeah."

He left without a backwards glance and the room felt empty and lacking as though he'd stripped it of any purpose.

Just a quick glimpse.

She looked around as though someone had said the words aloud. Maybe that wasn't such a bad idea. If she focused on the killer, on how they'd catch him, maybe she could *see* him. No. She'd promised herself. Nothing good ever happened when she opened up the future.

When her ability had begun to manifest just after her eighth birthday, no one knew what it would be. Foretelling had come first and her father had thought she might be able to manipulate or alter the future.

She'd told her mother about the strange waking dream she'd had about her uncle, her mother's only sibling. Erin had described the car accident that would take her uncle's life three days before it happened, right down to the fire that would make his remains difficult to identify.

Although Erin had only described the future, her mother had blamed her for causing it. Erin didn't understand her mother's withdrawal, then or now. Her parents' relationship, fragile on a good day, splintered and cracked. And then came the night her mother had left and her father hadn't stopped her. Erin began to notice the looks of the townspeople, heard the whispers. So she'd hidden her ability, had seldom used it at all until recently.

Use it. You were given this gift for a reason...to use it.

She gripped the sides of her head, fisting her hair. She didn't want to use it, didn't want to admit even to herself that she felt ugly and deformed for having it. It marked her as different. She'd tried so hard to fit in, to hide that part of herself.

The answers are in the future.

She wanted answers. Wanted them more than anything else. She'd been given this ability, this gift for a reason, to use it. The tension in her fingers pulled her hair tighter. The bite of pain punctured her thoughts. Wait. No. This wasn't her. These weren't her thoughts. The future never held answers, only pain, pain, and more pain. She pulled harder, the tautness making her scalp lift.

Look at the future. Her voice echoed words she knew

weren't hers. *The answers are there, waiting to be discovered.*

"No!"

She threw up a wall, visualizing as she'd been taught, a mental fortress that would block her aunt or anyone else from sneaking into her thoughts. The killer. He'd found a new way to get into her head. Was this how he'd been able to manipulate Greg and Keith by disguising his thoughts as theirs? They wouldn't have known how to block him or even be able to distinguish the difference between his words and theirs.

The fortress shook, but held. He kept trying to get at her. She focused all her energy into the force field and soon she could feel him retreating, slithering back to his cave of anonymity. Taking slow, deep breaths, she relaxed her fingers and slid them out of her hair and into her lap. She wasn't surprised to find strands trapped between her fingers. She took another breath and shivered, flicking off the last slivers of his control.

This had to stop. But how?

The idea she'd had earlier when Graham had come in and distracted her came back full force. What if she played his game? What if she let it be known that she'd seen the killer in a vision? What if *she* drew him out of hiding?

Revealing her secret would bring back all the whispers and stares of the townspeople. Could she do it? Was she ready to expose her secret and give up any hope of being normal, of being accepted? No one in this town would ever look at her the same way again. She'd never fit in.

She had to do it, had to save her dad and aunt. She had to stop this killer before he struck again.

GRAHAM STOOD next to Pax on the uneven pavement outside of Betty's Buds and Blooms on Main Street and watched the tow truck driver hook up Axel Freed's SUV.

"And he has no idea why he drove his car through the window?" Pax asked.

"Nope," Graham answered. "The idea just popped into his head."

"Is there a full moon or something?"

"Not that I know of."

"So many screwy things happening, like you shaving your beard. Erin make you do it?"

Graham shot Pax an annoyed look. "No."

"You wouldn't be the first guy to bend to the will of his woman." Pax held up his palms. "Just sayin'."

"You get the ballistics report back on the Hallowell shooting yet?"

"Not yet. Some foul up in the lab." Pax turned his focus back to the SUV tail up through the display window. "Your dad'll be glad…about the beard."

"I've got to get back to the station." Graham gestured toward the hysterical Betty, giving her account of what happened to another officer. "You got this?"

"Yeah. But—" Pax sidled up closer to Graham. "I gotta ask. Is it true?"

"Is what true?"

"That Erin has some kind of divining power."

"What? *Where* did you hear that?"

Pax had the good sense to look ashamed. "My wife."

"Who did she hear it from?"

"Her sister?"

"And who did her sister get it from?"

Tilting his head back, Pax looked up at the gray sky as if the answer were written there. He bunched up his face. "The lady who cuts her hair maybe?"

Graham spun on his heels and stalked toward the sheriff's station.

Pax followed. "So it is true."

"Shut up, Pax."

"I'll be damned. I just thought it was a bunch of gossipy women with nothing to do over there."

"Not another word."

"I always knew there was something off about her. Her whole family is whacked. I heard—"

Graham halted and spun on Pax. "I'll tell you what. Why don't you get Mabel to write up that flower shop accident back there? Then you could take over for her as the biggest gossipmonger in town."

"Hey."

"I don't know who started this stupid rumor, but it's going to end right here, got it?"

"Sure, Sheriff. Whatever you say."

Graham left Pax standing where he was and continued on to the station. What in the hell was wrong with this town? He didn't know what Erin would do when she found out about this latest development. Stupid, goddamned small town. He couldn't wait to...

shit. Who was he kidding? He was never leaving this town. Not with his parents the way they were and now his relationship with Erin. Plus it was clear this town needed a sheriff and for some reason it had been decided decades ago that the sheriff had to be a Doran.

He reached the top of the stairs of the front porch of the station and turned back to look up Main Street. Folks stood around, watching the tow truck operator and police do their jobs. Off to the side, the mayor huddled with his cronies, no doubt plotting their next move to get rid of him. They'd ratcheted up their recall campaign and now a few of the businesses in town sported flyers damning Graham as the worst thing to happen to San Rey since the storm that wiped out the original 1910 pier.

He turned his gaze away from Mayor Behre and his henchmen and scanned the other faces. He knew them all... Well, most of them anyway. He watched while Mr. Pasarelli passed out samples of cake from his bakery, trying to drum up business in the slow economy. He watched the Bercher boy swipe a second sample when Mr. Pasarelli's back was turned. The ladies from the Clippity-Do-Da talked to each other from behind their hands, no doubt passing more gossip and innuendo. A girl he'd gone to high school with passed her crying baby over to old Mrs. Gladstone who was known for her touch with fussy infants.

Just a normal town full of normal people in the middle of the most extraordinary and horrifying events of their lives. Between their neighborly smiles and nods of recognition, their brows knit in anxiety and confusion. What was happening to their town, their home? When would it end? Who would make it stop?

He would.

Graham pulled in a slow breath and squared his shoulders. He would. He would make it stop. He'd catch the asshole who was manipulating these good people to do strange and terrible things. And life in San Rey would go back to normal. A nice, boring normal where the worst thing that could happen would be that they'd run out of shortcake at the Strawberry Festival.

This was his town, his home. There was no way in hell he was going to let them down.

9

Word was definitely out if the glances and stares Erin was getting while shopping the aisles of Goldman's Drug Store were any indication. Mabel had done her job. Erin hoped her plan would work or else she'd exposed herself for nothing.

"...disgusting little weirdo, just like the rest of them."

Erin turned from perusing toothpaste to find Emily Talbot and Morgan Davies glaring at her.

"What are you looking at?" Emily sneered.

"She thinks she's so much better than us," Morgan said. "You use your woo-woo power to get the sheriff to screw you?"

"She'd have to. No other explanation for why he'd touch a freak like her."

Erin grabbed a box of toothpaste, threw it in her basket and bolted. The women's laughter reached out after her, scratching at old wounds. Her mother had used that word.

Freak.

She stumbled two rows over and grabbed onto an end-cap shelf. She'd expected curiosity, maybe even standoffishness, but aggression? No. None of that.

Hurrying toward the cash registers at the front of the store, she kept her head down, hoping to evade Emily and Morgan. She put her basket on the conveyor belt and waited for the man in front of her to finish paying. Mr. Felix, her third grade teacher, the man who had encouraged her in the months after her mother had left, now turned to look at her with a mixture of suspicion and revulsion.

She backed out of line right into Candy. "Oh. Sorry."

"Sorry? You're *sorry*? Watch where you're going!"

Erin sucked in a breath at the hatred coming off her friend and hairstylist. Suddenly the whispers were everywhere, the stares fixed and accusatory. *Weirdo. Freak. Monster.* Erin brushed past Candy, bumping into a display and scattering it. Then she ran, passing face after face twisted in hatred. Their loathing followed her like a rabid dog.

She dove into her car and slammed the door, her breath harsh in the quiet. Her worst nightmare had come true. They were all against her. The whole town. She'd never fit in now. All her life she'd only wanted to fit into the town she belonged to and now...now that wish would never come true. What had she done? It wasn't supposed to be like this.

Her phone rang, startling her. She fumbled around in her purse until she finally located it.

"Hello?"

"What did you do?"

Graham. Oh, God. Not him too.

"Why did you tell Mabel about your ability?" he demanded.

"What?"

"Why, Erin? You had to know she'd tell everybody." He let out a heavy breath. "That was the point, wasn't it?"

She dropped her head back against the headrest. "We have to catch him."

"*We* don't have to do anything. You work for a property management company, not the sheriff's office. Goddammit. What if he came after you physically like he did Deidre?"

She wasn't an idiot. She'd considered the probability that the killer could come after her the way he'd come after Deidre. He'd already attacked her and her family mentally and it was clear he wouldn't stop. She didn't like hearing the fear in Graham's voice, but what choice was there? How else were they going to stop him?

"He might," she said, closing her eyes against that thought.

"And what? You don't care?"

"He's already come at me, into my head."

"That's not the same as coming at you with a gun. You can't fight off a bullet with a little mental gymnastics."

"I just want my dad and aunt back."

He gentled his tone. "I know you do, Babe. Where are you?"

She glanced around at the parking lot of the strip mall. People came and went, going about their day as though nothing was wrong. "Shopping."

"Come to the station."

"Why? So you can yell at me some more?"

"Erin, just come. Please."

"No more yelling at me."

"I can't promise that, but I'll try."

"All right." She clicked her phone closed with a sigh and tossed it into her purse. At least Graham hadn't turned against her. She had one person on her side. The most important person.

It was a short drive to the station and in no time, she parked and went inside. Jessica had the phone pressed between her ear and shoulder while she filed her nails. Mabel had called in to stay with Erin's father, which was where Erin had found her that morning when she'd spilled her secret about her ability. If only she could go back in time. But then what was the alternative?

Jessica hung up the phone. "Well, if it isn't Witchy Woman. Now I know how you managed to land Graham."

"I don't have that kind of ability."

Jessica rose from her chair and came around the desk. "He's not going to want you when he finds out what you are, you know."

"He already knows."

"Yeah, right."

"Is he here?"

"He's busy." Jessica planted her hands on her hips. "Why don't you go practice your voodoo on someone else?"

"Knock it off, Jessica," Graham said.

Erin jumped at the sound of his voice. "Jeez. You scared me."

Graham put a hand on Erin's low back. "Sorry."

"How can you touch her?" Jessica asked, disgust evident in her expression and words. "Don't you know what she is?"

"I said to knock it off."

"How clever of you," Jessica taunted, edging toward them. "You put a hex on him so he can't see what you are. But I see. I know."

Jessica's reaction was more than unexpected. It was extreme, over the top. Could this too be the killer's doing?

Erin drew closer to Graham. "Stop it."

"Murderer," Jessica sneered, her lip curling as she stalked closer.

Graham wrapped his arm around Erin. "No more, Jessica. Not another word."

"She was at the house," Jessica continued. "I bet she's the one who killed Deidre and Greg. And how convenient." Jessica stood just inches away now. "Using your powers to mess with the sheriff's head. I bet you made Keith kill himself. Got rid of the obstacle in your path to Graham." Jessica leaned in and Erin could see the fever in her eyes just like the one that burned behind her father's gaze. "You're not going to get rid of me. He's mine!"

She lunged for Erin. Graham put a hand out to stop her, but Jessica got in one good swipe before he hauled Erin back. Erin gripped her cheek where Jessica had dug her nails in. The gashes burned. Erin backed away, shaking. Jessica was shrieking now, struggling against Graham's hold to get to Erin.

"Go," Graham told her. "I'll take care of Jessica. Go home. I'll call you."

Erin snatched her purse up from where it had fallen when Jessica had attacked her. Her head ached from fighting back the tears, but she managed to stumble down the steps to her car.

"Monster!" someone shouted, drawing her attention to the crowd gathering.

"Witch!"

"Freak!"

Someone grabbed her elbow. She spun, ready to strike.

"You'd better get," Graham's father said, his fingers biting into her flesh. "Go someplace else. Move to another town, another state. Stay away from my son."

She jerked her arm free and ran to her car. As she pulled away she thought she saw Ham smile, all teeth, his stare flat and penetrating right into the center of her chest. She hit the gas, leaving behind the town she'd once loved, the town she'd tried so hard to fit into.

GRAHAM WRESTLED Jessica into her chair and leaned over her, bracketing her with his hands on the arms of the chair. "You're lucky I don't lock you up for assault."

"She deserved it."

"What in the hell is wrong with everybody in this town?"

"We're finally seeing her and her family for what they are. You don't want her, Graham." She ran her hands up Graham's arms and locked them behind his neck, trying to draw him down to her. "You want me." She licked her lips. "I know how to make a man feel good. Real good."

Graham pulled his head back and tried to move away, but she hung on, yanking him toward her. He had no choice but to grab onto her to keep them both from going down.

"What's going on here?" Ham shouted.

Jessica wriggled closer, pulling Graham's head down, aiming for a kiss.

Graham clamped a hand over her mouth and pushed her head back just before she connected. "I have no idea. This whole town has gone completely insane."

"You'd better not be using your position as sheriff to cut a swath through the women in this town." Ham shook his finger at his son, his face flushed and sweaty. "I raised you to respect the union between a man and a woman."

Jessica licked Graham's palm, drawing his attention away from his father. "Stop that!"

Jessica grinned at him from behind his hand and ground her pelvis into Graham's.

"Graham Doran! You stop that cavorting right now!"

"I'm not cavorting. She is." Graham grabbed Jessica's wandering hands and pulled them behind her back. "I said stop it!" he told her. She was like a goddamned octopus. Every time he thought he had her under control, she seemed to grow another arm to go after him again.

"But Graham, baby, I want you so bad." She rubbed her breasts against his chest. "You want me too. I know it."

"No, actually, I don't. What I want is for you to sit back down at your desk and do your job."

Jessica tried to rub up on him again, but this time he managed to move out of the way. "That's it." He spun her around, pushed her down on the desk, and clamped handcuffs on her wrists. He held her down by the back of the neck. "There."

"Oohhh, dirty," Jessica cooed. "I like it." She widened her legs, wiggling her ass. "Frisk me, sheriff. *All* over. Go deep."

"Goddammit, Jessica. Knock it off!"

"Watch your language," Ham scolded, vibrating so hard he wobbled. "It's bad enough I have to witness your depravity, but I will not have you use the Lord's name in vain." Ham caught himself on the edge of a desk. "Do you hear me?" Graham made a move to go to his father, but Ham put a hand up. "Just take care of your problem."

Graham eyed his father, trying to gauge how much

discomfort his old man was in. He knew Ham tried to hide the effects of his illness. For any of it to show, as it did now, meant that his dad was using every available scrap of energy just to stay upright.

"Sorry, Pop." Graham hauled Jessica up to stand. "I'll be right back." He propelled her forward toward the cells at the back of the station.

Jessica tried to break free when she caught on to where they were headed. "Come on, Graham, honey. I was just joking. You know me. I'm always kidding around." She went lax in his grip and would've fallen if he hadn't had such a firm hold on her. "Please, Graham. Don't do this," she whined, fighting harder against him. "I love you. Please."

"You're only going to hurt yourself if you keep struggling."

He managed to get her into the only available cage, uncuffed her, and escaped before she could scramble out after him.

She grabbed the bars and shook them. "Graham. Come on, baby. Let me out. Fun's over. I promise to be good." Her expression changed from pleading to seductive. "I'll be real good. I'll be so good you'll scream when you come. Promise."

He turned his back on her, curling his lip in disgust. She was young, too young, to be talking like that. What in the hell had come over her? She'd always had a schoolgirl crush on him, he knew, and he made sure he did nothing to encourage her. But something, no, someone had turned the heat up to boiling.

"Graham! Graham!"

He closed the door on Jessica and took a slow, deep breath that brought with it thoughts of Erin. The look of horror on Erin's face as Jessica had lunged for her... She'd come in so pale and fragile-looking and then Jessica had lost her shit and gone after her. If Jessica had been a man, he'd have punched her in the face. He needed to see Erin to make sure she was okay. But first he had to deal with his dad.

He found Ham slumped in one of the lobby chairs, his face pasty and damp.

"Pop!" He rushed to his father's side. "Are you all right?" He felt his father's pulse, weak and thready. "I'm calling an ambulance."

Ham gripped Graham's wrist harder than he thought was possible in the condition his father was in. "No," Ham rasped. "Just a moment...to rest."

"Not this time." He started to rise, but Ham held fast.

"No."

"Pop, you've got to stop stressing yourself like this. It's not good for you."

"You shaved." Ham reached up with his other hand and gave Graham's face a weak pat. "'Bout time."

Damn, but his pop was a stubborn old man. Graham couldn't help the smile that tugged at the corner of his mouth. "I didn't do it for you."

"Don't care."

"No more talking." Graham took the chair next to Ham. "Can I get you some water?"

Ham rolled his head back and forth against the wall. Color was starting to creep into his cheeks and he wasn't struggling for every breath as he had been. Still, Graham worried. Seeing his father weak shook something low inside him. His parents had always been his rock and now his mother's sifting memory and his father's frailness had cracked the foundation of his life.

"Let me take you home," Graham said.

"In a minute." Ham took a handkerchief out and dabbed his forehead. His gaze roamed the station. "Wasn't much older than you...when I took over for my father. This place...this town...it's who we are."

"Don't talk. Catch your breath."

"No." Ham turned his sharp stare on his son. "I'm going to say this...and hope you hear me this time. You have a legacy...not many people can say that. Six generations of Dorans have protected this town. Do you understand what that means?" Ham didn't wait for a response. "This town is our blood, sweat, and tears. It's our children...and our children's children. It's more than a century of shielding San Rey...from the evil that lurks inside and out.

"We're guardians of this town...and everything it stands for. Without us...well, you've seen what happens. Lawlessness, immorality, greed...they grow and fester, rotting away our very souls. We're the soldiers who stand guard. We're the shield between good and evil. Do you understand?"

Did he understand? Graham had only heard this speech a thousand times growing up. It had been drilled into him from the cradle. He could recite it by heart the way school kids could recite the Pledge of Allegiance. But until today, when he'd stood on the porch of the station and looked out on the town he'd been born to protect, the words had rung hollow. Today, suddenly, they filled up, and he felt each one of them as though they'd been carved into his DNA. He was the guardian of this town. He was the one chosen to protect it. And he'd do everything in his power to fulfill his duty.

"Yes, Pop," he answered quietly. "I understand."

Ham studied him. Looked right into his eyes, right into the center of his chest. And tears welled in Ham's eyes. "Yes. You do. You finally do."

He'd never seen his father cry, had hardly ever seen him touched by softer emotions. Graham held his father's gaze, ignoring the lump that had formed in his throat and the burning at the backs of his own eyes.

"I'm proud of you, son," Ham said and that lump turned into a boulder. "You'll do fine. You'll do us proud."

"Thank you."

Ham gave a firm nod and cleared his throat. "There's just one thing left."

"What's that?"

"You have to get rid of that December girl."

ERIN SAT at her aunt's bedside, the steady blips on the monitor the only movement in the room. She'd come here seeking solace, but holding her aunt's hand, she felt everything but relief. Even if her plan eventually worked and she managed to draw out the killer, her life in San Rey was over. She'd only been kidding herself thinking she could belong. She was the square peg that would never fit. None of them had, not her aunt nor her father. She saw that now. They'd only pretended, all the while she'd been looking in from the outside.

Where would she go? What would she do? She supposed she could get a job somewhere else, sell her house and move. She'd never considered living anywhere else but San Rey and now that the world was opened to her, it was all so overwhelming, the vastness of it a black yawning gap laid out before her.

Maybe she could move to Los Angeles with Graham. They'd get an apartment together, build a life. He could get his job back with the LAPD. She could get a job at another property management company. Maybe they'd get married, have kids. The world outside didn't seem so scary, imagining Graham at her side.

But that would mean leaving her aunt and dad. Although after everything they've been through, they might not want to stay in San Rey either.

She searched her aunt's face for some kind of change. Nothing. The doctors were still stumped about what to do for her, other than keep her sedated. She'd lost weight. Her skin hung a little looser and she was so pale. Fine lines that hadn't been there a few weeks ago added years Cerie didn't get to live. Erin ran her thumb across the back of her aunt's hand. The veins stood proud, like the blue roots of a water-starved tree.

"Please come back to me," she begged, holding Cerie's hand to her face. "I need you. You always know what to say, what I need to hear. I feel so lost without you."

Her plea met a silence that roared in her ears. Seeing her aunt this way was like losing her mother all over again. What would she do if Cerie never recovered? The vibrant woman who'd taught Erin how to use and control her ability was now imprisoned within her own. She reached out to Cerie with her mind, searching for that metaphysical link they'd always shared. But it was like reaching out blindly in a dark room, swiping at air over and over again. The link was gone. Cut by unseen hands.

She pushed to her feet. That was it. She wasn't going to let some chickenshit invisible asshole do this to her family. She was going to fight back and fight back hard.

"I'll find out who he is. I'll find him and stop him." She gave her aunt's papery cheek a quick kiss. "Hang in there for me."

She left without looking back. There was only one direction to move in now.

10

Graham had been called away to handle three more incidents since his father left. He was neck deep in paperwork that would take weeks to dig through, but at least Jessica had finally cooled off enough in her cell that he felt confident enough to let her loose and send her home. She'd seemed genuinely embarrassed and bewildered at her own behavior. He'd accepted every single one of her twenty red-faced apologies before he finally shoved her out the door and told her he'd see her tomorrow.

This was after going thirty rounds with his father over Erin. No matter how many times his father had come at him, threatened him, cajoled him, he'd held firm. The only way he'd give Erin up was if *she* called things off. And Graham hoped to God that would never happen.

His old man had finally given up the fight and left, refusing a ride home from him out of spite. He wasn't sure if Ham would ever speak to him again. Well, he just wouldn't give him a choice. Whether his father liked it or not, he and his mother needed him. Ham could be as angry as he wanted. Graham wasn't going to budge on this. He hated to think it, but Ham was too sick to do much about it anyway. And with his brother Adam away, Graham was all they had.

Ham would get used to him being with Erin. Eventually. Maybe. Hopefully.

Sitting at his desk in his finally quiet office, Graham realized it was already full dark outside and he hadn't heard back from Erin. He pulled out his phone. No new messages. His first attempt to reach her got her voice mail so he'd texted her. No response.

Was she pissed off at him about Jessica? He thought back to earlier in the afternoon when he'd told her to leave after Jessica had attacked her. He went through everything he'd said and done. He'd been abrupt, maybe a little rude. He'd only been trying to get Jessica to settle the hell down. Erin wasn't so sensitive that she'd stop taking his calls.

He tried calling again and left a message this time. Maybe he'd just go over to her house with a pizza and a bottle of wine. She couldn't stay annoyed at him forever. He'd find a way to talk her out of it if she tried. As he shut down his computer, another thought struck him. What if she couldn't answer her phone? What if her plan had worked and the killer had gone after her?

He didn't wait to make sure the program he was working in closed before he bolted out the door.

ERIN WASN'T sure what had drawn her to the bluffs above San Rey where she and Graham had first kissed. The night air bit through her lightweight coat and she shivered. Seeing her aunt had steadied her in a way she hadn't felt in days. Weeks. If only she'd open her eyes. If only her father could speak again. If only things could go back to normal.

Normal.

What was normal anymore?

She wrapped her arms around herself and looked out at the sea, stretching before her. The moon hung low in the sky, laying out a path of light across the water that nearly led all the way to the rocks below her. Standing at the edge, she had the feeling she could fly, soar over the dark ocean, dipping down and up again. She closed her eyes and imagined it. The wind lifted the ends of her hair, bringing with it a fine salty mist that dampened her cheeks.

Her feet crept closer to the edge. The sensation of flying was so real to her now that her stomach lifted and sank as she imagined rising swiftly then dropping down to skim the waves. Her problems melted away, trailing out behind her in a long tail. Freedom. The ocean called to her. Called her by name in a low, sweet, seductive voice. She inched a little closer and tried to answer.

Suddenly she popped her eyes open. Her toes met the edge of the cliff and the sea no longer called. The voice was not some ethereal being, but a real life, flesh and blood human. And he was right behind her.

Her feet felt as though they were bolted to the earth and she had to twist her body to look at him. Her breath got sucked away, making her jerk back. She wobbled.

"Not yet," Ham said and she righted as though he'd reached his hand out and stilled her.

Ham sat on the bench where she'd first felt a real, definable connection to Graham. His back pressed into the wooden slats, as though he needed them to keep upright. Sallow light from the street lamp above him cast a dirty halo around his head. He reached for every breath like the backlash of a whip, his body yanking and sagging. She could feel his oily, black loathing coating her. He clutched the head of his cane, another anchor, his leather gloves squeaking in time with her heartbeats.

The vision. Her hands, but not her hands. The squeak of leather gloves, gripping the handle of the gun outside Deidre's backdoor, and again as he shot Deidre. The annoyance. The anger. The shame. She shuddered, bile rising up her throat. This was the man who'd killed Deidre. And Greg. And Keith. This was the monster who'd trapped her aunt and father inside their own minds, turning them into nothing more than shells.

She thought of Graham. This would break him. His father had been behind everything all along, every manipulation. The cruelty of his betrayal struck like a blow to the stomach. What would this do to Graham after what he'd been through with Patricia? She wished she could shield him from the pain of the truth.

"Why?" Was all she could think to say.

"You lied."

His tone bit into her. She shook her head. "Lied?"

"You have a power. Or was that the real lie?"

"I saw you."

"Saw." Squeak. Squeak. "What exactly did you *see*?"

"I saw you kill Deidre. I saw you make Greg shoot himself. I saw you force Keith to tie his own noose and...and hang himself."

"You didn't see me. You saw what I can *do*." He sucked in a breath. "You saw power."

Her head crowded with what he'd done, what he was willing to do, and how he tried to impress her with it. Her face flushed hot and her vision narrowed on him. "I saw cowardice!"

"You want to see...exactly what I can do, little girl? I'm holding you on the edge." He flicked a finger in her direction. Even that small movement seemed an effort for him. "One flick and you go."

Maybe if she pushed at him. "You got Deidre pregnant. Does your wife know about that?"

"You don't talk about my wife!" he wheezed and tipped to one side.

She felt her right foot slide out an inch. Looking down, she watched as pebbles bounced and danced down the cliff face. She curled her toes, trying to grip the earth.

"I'm sorry." She hated the panic in her voice and tried to steady her breathing. "I won't talk about her."

Turning away from the vast darkness below, she saw him brace against his cane, attempting to right himself. She waited, trying to mentally push back on the strange hold he had on her. She'd been so shocked to see him that her mind had opened all its doors to him. He'd slipped right in. And now that he was there, she was having a hard time driving him out.

"You're sick," she tried. "You need a doctor."

He managed to correct himself, listing a little to the left. "Nothing a doctor can do."

"Your ability—"

"Power."

"Power." She hated that word. She hated him. "How does it work?" Maybe if she distracted him with flattery, she'd find a way to gain back some control.

"I'm an Influencer...from a long line of Influencers."

"You influence what? People's thoughts? Their actions?"

"Both. We were crowd control. Mostly. Only...I found a way to enhance my God given power. Amplify it. Narrow it. Like a laser. All at will."

What he did was anything but godly. He enjoyed his *power*, actually liked hurting people. She could feel the sick glee radiating off him. Her stomach churned with the thought of all he'd done. But that pleasure came with a price.

"It costs you to use it."

"Side effect of the medication," he huffed. "It passes."

She thought of what Graham had told her about his father getting worse and worse. And how sick he'd become over the last few weeks. "Does it? Seems to me you're getting worse."

He scowled at her. "You question me?"

She felt her foot slide a little further over the edge. Half an inch, but enough that she couldn't balance on both feet anymore. Pushing back at the searing panic, she swallowed hard and scrambled to get her emotions in check. She needed all of her mental strength to fight him off, to regain control of her own body from him.

"No," she answered an octave too high. "I'm just concerned for you. Graham's been so worried."

"I warned him to stay away from you." His chest heaved with each breath. "He wouldn't listen. Whores. All of you. Tempting men...into evil."

He'd put her into the same category he'd put Deidre. When she'd flashed back to Deidre's murder, he'd blamed Deidre for his fall from grace, for making him break his marriage vows with her. And he saw Erin as the whore who'd bring Graham down. She knew then he was going to kill her. Get rid of her as he'd gotten rid of Deidre. Redoubling her efforts to get free, she closed her eyes and pushed back against him. If... she...could...just...break...his...control...

"I can feel you. You think you can resist me?" His laugh chopped at her, cutting into her concentration. "I'm too powerful now."

Everywhere she turned were invisible walls, trapping her in. She couldn't find a weakness. All her efforts only seemed to strengthen his hold on her. The harder she fought back, the closer the walls moved in on her until she couldn't even raise her arms. She was suffocating, her chest heaving as she fought for each breath. He struggled just as hard, his efforts to entrap her having the same effect on him.

"You're a coward," she spat out. "You disgust me."

"My son will think...you killed yourself...couldn't handle the whole town...hating you."

He smiled a sickly smile and she knew he'd done that too, turned the whole town against her. She never knew anyone could be so evil, so disgustingly power hungry.

"He'll know I didn't."

"Won't matter."

"He loves me." It was the only weapon she had against him. "And I love him."

"Love." He said the word as though it was excrement he'd scraped off his shoe. "You're nothing...but a good time. He'll come to see that."

"He'll never forgive you."

"He'll never know. But...if he should...he'll one day thank me."

His words didn't match his tone. She studied him. His face was paler now and he shook like an addict denied his fix. And then it hit her.

"You're afraid of me."

He narrowed his eyes at her. "Don't be stupid."

"Oh, my god. You are. You're afraid of me. That's why you want to get rid of me. I saw you. I saw what you are."

"Do not use the Lord's name in vain!"

He pitched forward, clutching at his chest. At the same time she felt her foot slide out from under her and go over the edge. Her balance knocked off, she hit the ground hard. He wheezed and coughed, both hands gripping his chest.

"I'm sorry!" She dug her fingers into the rocky soil, clawing for purchase. Her leg was a dead weight, pulling her down. "I won't do it ever again. I promise. Please!"

He rolled his head back and grinned at her, a sick twisted smile that made her weak with panic. He wouldn't make it fast. He'd draw it out, make her beg and cry. She was already crying, already begging, hot tears dripping into the dark earth. She bowed her head and thought of Graham. He'd find her broken body on the jagged rocks below. He'd blame himself. She couldn't do that to him, couldn't let him carry around more guilt.

"I love him," she whispered into the dirt. "He loves me. I love him and he loves me." She raised her head and looked right at Ham, daring him with her declaration. "I love him and he loves me." As she said it, she sent out a call to Graham, pushed all her love for him out into the universe. "I love him and he loves me." She repeated it over and over, growing louder and louder until her love for him became a thing she could feel all around her.

Ham reared back against the bench seat. He stared at her in horror. She clawed her way toward him, defying him to stop her.

"I love him. And he loves me. And there's nothing you can do about it. You're weak and pathetic. Look at you!" She gained her feet slowly, rising to stand. "You use your ability to hurt and kill and it's killing you. It's killing you."

"Shut up!" Spittle dotted his chin and his eyes narrowed into thin black slits. He heaved himself up from the bench with more energy than she thought he had left. He raised a crooked finger at her. "The only one dying tonight is *you*."

11

Graham stood on Erin's doorstep, just stood there. He couldn't move, couldn't even raise his hand to knock. She called to him, the sound carried to him on the night wind. He strained to listen, thinking at first he might be imagining it. Terror hit him like a gunshot to the chest. His knees buckled. Catching the door handle, he used it to keep upright.

"Erin!"

He could feel her, her shock, her anger, her fear. And then a wave of love washed over all of it, swelling until it filled him up. He pushed away from the door, suddenly freed, and climbed back into his car. He started the engine, not knowing which way to go. All he knew was that he had to get to her.

He found himself taking the turns up to the bluffs a little too fast, and forced himself to slow even though everything in him screamed at him to hurry. He parked and climbed out of the car. He could see her now, lying in the dirt. A man stood over her. He couldn't quite process what he was seeing.

"Pop?"

Ham turned toward him. One look and Graham knew his dad was in trouble. He looked like he was going to pass out any moment.

"Pop!" He rushed toward his father, but Ham put up a hand.

"Graham," Erin gasped, looking up at him from his father's feet. "Be careful."

Careful? "What in the hell is going on here?"

"Graham—"

"Shut up!" Ham shouted down at her.

Erin flinched as though Ham had hit her. She turned toward Graham, her lips pressed hard together, her nostrils flaring. She glanced up sharply at Ham, then back at him. Graham shook his head, trying to get a grasp on what the hell was happening.

"She's no good for you, son."

"Erin, are you hurt?"

Erin shook her head, her mouth a firm, flat line. She jerked her head toward his car. She wanted him to leave? What in the hell?

"Somebody tell me what's going on right now."

He glanced from Erin to his father and back again. Her eyes were wide with fear and something else, something shocking and seething. The truth. The realization broke hot over him like a scorching bath, leaving behind a bitter, unbelievable revelation.

He swung his gaze back up to his father who was shaking as though weak from illness, but as he looked closer, he saw what had been there the whole time, and he *knew*.

"It was you."

"Now that you've accepted your role...your heritage...you will be the true sheriff of this town."

"You killed them." Even as he said the words, everything in him worked to reject them. He couldn't believe his father capable. He wanted his father to deny it, to explain everything away, to point the finger elsewhere.

"I did what was necessary," Ham wheezed, the arm that gripped his cane shaking.

What was necessary? As though killing was nothing more than a household chore to him. He looked at Ham, seeing him as if for the first time. A fissure broke open in his chest, dividing him into two parts. The part of him that still wanted to believe in his father and the part of him that knew him for the monster he was. A murderer.

"You killed Deidre." *Jesus.* "You got her pregnant and killed her. Then you killed Greg and made it look like he killed Deidre. And Keith..." A sick knot formed in his gut. "How could you?"

"With true power comes responsibility. I'll teach you as my father taught me. You'll be the greatest Influencer yet."

Graham jerked back as his father's words truly sank in. Power. Heritage. Influencer. Ham wanted his son to be like him, like his father and his father before him and so on, going back six generations. Murder and manipulation were in his blood, sewn into his genes.

"Didn't you ever wonder," Ham asked, his tone

conversational, "why your confession rate was the highest in the precinct? How you could talk anyone into anything? How if you really put your mind to it, you could have anything you wanted?"

Ham looked down at Erin. "How you could get this one to drop her boyfriend and fall flat on her back for you?" Ham turned his gaze back to his son. "That's your heritage, son. We're Influencers. Protectors of this town."

Graham stumbled back a step, a guttural moan ripped from his chest. *No!* Everything in his life, everything he'd ever thought he'd worked for, every person he'd met, every job he had, every case he'd solved, every woman he'd ever taken to bed...had any of that been real? Had he earned even one success? Or had it all come from his ability to manipulate people to do what he wanted?

"No," Graham whispered. The enormity of everything in his life being stripped away from him brought him to his knees.

And Erin too. Was what they'd shared even real? Had she confided in him because she'd trusted him or because he'd unknowingly compelled her to do it? Had she gone to bed with him because she wanted him or was it because *he* wanted *her*? Had he, in a sense, raped her?

"No," he moaned, dropping to all fours in the rocky soil. He couldn't catch his breath. Blackness crowded his vision. He gripped the soil, the rocks biting into his flesh the only real things left for him.

His father's feet appeared in his hazed line of sight.

"You'll come to accept your power, develop it, and use it. I'll teach you as my father taught me."

"I don't want it!"

"How could you not want your God given gift? How could you not grow it and use it as He intended?"

"God given?" Graham staggered to his feet, a rising, churning tide of anger swelling within him. "What you did was not sanctioned by God or anyone else. You killed people. You killed your own child!"

"Grown or not, you don't get to talk to me like that." Ham reached out to put a shaky hand on Graham's shoulder. "Son—"

Graham jerked away. "Don't call me that. Don't ever touch me again."

"You don't mean that." Ham took a wobbly step forward. "You're in shock. I was just like you—"

"You're *nothing* like me." He couldn't believe this was the man who'd raised him. Who'd showed him how to shoot a gun, catch a pass, and build a fort. The man who'd taught him right from wrong, for fuck's sake.

He turned away from his father and caught sight of Erin still on the ground as though she was injured or couldn't get up. His face burned with shame. He'd never be able to look her in the eye again, knowing he'd taken away her free will. He'd never be able to hold her and kiss her without wondering if she really welcomed his attentions. Wiping the back of his hand across his mouth, he swallowed back the vomit that climbed the back of his throat.

He moved toward Erin and knelt down. He wanted

to touch her, hold her, and tell her everything would be all right. But he no longer had the right. He balled his fists at his sides. "Are you okay?"

Her lips were still pressed together as though glued shut. He realized that she'd hardly moved an inch since he'd arrived.

He turned back to his father, pointing at Erin. "What have you done to her?"

"Go home, son. Let me deal with this."

"Release her. Now!"

"I'm not going to do that. Our legacy is a closely guarded secret. I can't let her go. She's your Eve. She'll tempt you away from your true purpose, your calling."

Graham lunged at his father, grasping the man's shirt in his fists. "Let her go or I swear to God—"

"Do not use the Lord's name in vain!" Ham gasped, his cheeks flamed red, his eyes bulging and red-rimmed.

Graham shook him. "Let her go!"

"No. Go home."

And then he knew. Ham was going to kill Erin. His skin was suddenly too tight to contain the rage that boiled and swelled within him. Before he realized what he meant to do, he'd pulled his gun and pointed it at Ham's head. He pressed it against the man's temple.

"Let. Her. Go."

Ham's eyes widened and he went a slack. "Son—"

He twisted his fist, bunching Ham's shirt tighter against his throat. "I told you not to call me that anymore," he said, pushing the words through gritted teeth. "You're nothing to me."

"You...you don't mean that. You're just—"

"Don't tell me what I am! You don't get to tell me anything ever again." He brought Ham closer, raising him up by the shirt until Ham's feet barely touched the ground. "Let her go. Now!"

Erin gasped for breath behind him. It was the sweetest sound he'd ever heard.

"You're making...a mistake," Ham panted. "She knows too much. She knows our secret."

He pressed the nozzle of the gun harder against Ham's temple. "My only mistake was believing in you."

"Graham." Erin's voice was weak, but brought a flood of relief to him.

She was all right.

"I'm still your father," Ham rasped.

"You're nothing but a lying, cheating murderer."

Erin struggled to her feet. With one hand pressed to her neck, she put a gentle hand on Graham's shoulder. "Graham."

He flinched from the contact. He'd never really be sure if her touch was real, if anything between them was or would ever be real. Ham's revelation had stripped him of everything. He'd never be able to do anything, get close to anyone without wondering if it was really his or not.

"Go home, Erin."

"I can't."

He couldn't see her, but he knew she was crying. He fought the urge to pull her into his arms by twisting a little harder on Ham's shirt. Ham's cane clattered to the ground as he grabbed Graham's wrist. Graham didn't want Erin to see him like this. She must already think him a monster, wondering the same things he had about their relationship, doubting everything they'd shared.

"I need him to...to release my dad and my aunt," she said.

"Do it," he ordered Ham. "Now."

Ham gasped like a landed fish, his face mottled and strained. "No."

He yanked on Ham's shirt. "I said, do it!"

Ham glared at him for a moment and then sagged, his eyes rolling back into his head. Graham scrambled to catch him before they both went down, dropping his gun to catch the back of Ham's head. He lowered Ham to the ground.

Erin knelt beside him. He still couldn't bring himself to look at her.

"He can't die," she said on a sob. "He has to release my aunt and my dad."

Graham checked Ham's pulse, his own battering out a hard rhythm. It was weak, but there. He let out a relieved breath. It was sick, but no matter what the man had done Graham couldn't bring himself to wish for his death. He pulled out his cell phone to call an ambulance. Erin put a hand on his arm. Her touch felt wrong. He stood and moved away to make the call, not wanting her to see how much it killed him to have her near and not be able to touch her.

Ending the call, he looked out over the ocean, everything in him churning and crashing like the waves below. He bent over, gripping his knees, trying to catch his breath. He'd pulled his gun on his own father, so close to pulling the trigger, he could almost hear the gunshot, imagine Ham's head jerking back, and the acrid smell of gunpowder and death.

Erin laid her hand on his back. He shrugged her off and moved away, out of reach. He wished she'd stop doing that. It hurt too much.

ERIN DIDN'T KNOW how to reach Graham. Every attempt she made, he rejected. She knew a little something about what he was going through. She'd been through it herself when she'd first come into her ability and her father explained how everyone in their family had some kind of ability. She'd never imagined there could be another family like hers in San Rey.

Graham kept his distance, his gaze moving past her to his father, then back out at the ocean. He wouldn't look at her or acknowledge her. She ached for him.

"It's not your fault," she said, trying to reach him. "He fooled all of us."

"Go home, Erin."

His rejection stung. She reached out to touch him, then pulled the gesture. He'd only shrug it off. Again.

"I'm not leaving you like this."

"Go home. I don't want you here." His words didn't match his tone.

She moved in front of him, forcing him to look at her. "I'm not leaving you. You need me."

"What I need is for you to go home. Now."

"I'm not leaving. I care about you, Graham."

"Do you? How can you be sure?"

"What's that supposed to mean?"

"How can you be sure about anything with me?"

"What?" Her confusion slowly morphed into understanding. His ability. He thought... *Oh, my god.*

He broke into her thoughts. "Did you want to tell me about your ability?"

"No, not at first, but you convinced—"

"I convinced you to tell me," he finished for her. "And when you kissed me that first time, was it because you wanted to?"

"Of course."

"Really? Because I really wanted you to kiss me. That's all I could think about that night when I came up here and found you. You kissing me. And then you did."

"Graham—"

"And when we had sex—" he broke off and rubbed the back of his hand over his mouth. "Did you really want to?"

"You can't... Yes. God, yes. I wanted you so bad."

"Really? Because I wanted you. I really, really wanted you. But most of all, I wanted you to want me. More than Keith, more than anyone you'd ever been with."

The anguish in his voice broke her heart. She couldn't help the tears that fell, couldn't stop the need to go to him and wrap her arms around him. He stiffened in her embrace, turning his head away, his jaw clenched.

"I wanted you more than anything," she whispered

fiercely, clinging harder to him even as he held his arms tight at his sides. "I want you now. I can't imagine a day going by when I wouldn't want you, when I wouldn't love you."

He finally looked at her, his gaze hot and searching. He started to say something.

Her body jolted.

A sharp pain punctured her shoulder, spinning her away from him.

The firecracker sound came late, just as he reached for her. The pain hit again, this time in her hip. The ground flew up towards her. Graham caught her, hanging her back over his arm. She heard another shot, this one not for her.

"Graham!" she shouted as the sky went black.

12

Graham expected to feel something. Anything. But the void that had punctured his chest when Erin was shot radiated out, spreading through every cell in his body, as though he could not only feel nothing, he *was* nothing. Watching the medical team work over Ham's body, making a valiant effort at keeping the old man alive, he stood at the foot of the hospital bed and tried with every part of him to think *nothing.*

If Ham died, it would be from the bullets Graham had put in him and not because Graham had inadvertently used his ability wishing for Ham's heart to just...stop.

He didn't have to close his eyes to recall the way Erin's body had jerked, the way her eyes had widened and her lips had parted as the first bullet hit. Something in him—training, muscle memory—recognized what was happening before his brain could wrap around it, and he was already going for his back up piece as he threw an arm out to catch her. And then the gun was in his hand, his finger pulling the trigger when the second bullet hit her.

He didn't remember the sound of his gun firing. Erin's scream had filled his head, blocking every other sound out, including whatever it was his father had said in that last instant before Graham's finger had fully depressed the trigger. Then, again. And again. Until it clicked empty and Ham lay motionless.

Graham had had to replay everything for Pax and somehow explain to the now acting sheriff why Ham would shoot Erin and why he would empty his gun into his own father. He couldn't exactly tell Pax what Ham had done or about Erin, the abilities, and the shit storm that was now his life. So he told a half-truth about Ham thinking Erin wasn't good enough for Graham and about how Ham's illness had changed him mentally.

Graham crossed his arms over his chest and balled his fists. His shirt was stiff with Erin's blood mixed with Ham's. The metallic stench of it made his stomach twist into a sick knot. He swallowed to keep from gagging.

The monitor went from blips to a scream, yanking Graham's attention back to the bed and the man lying in it.

"He's crashing!"

Graham was ignored as the team went to work restarting Ham's heart. Again. Siphoning his focus entirely from the room, his thoughts went to Erin two floors up in surgery. She'd been covered in blood that had just kept coming. He'd held her hand in the ambulance, pressing it to his forehead and willing her to live with everything in him. He couldn't lose her. Not now. Not like this.

A hand on his arm wrenched him back from his thoughts. He tried to focus on the doctor's face, thinking he should at least make an effort to remember what she looked like as she told him that the man who had once been his father was dead.

GOD, she hurt. All over. Even her hair hurt. She lay back, absorbing the pain, trying to sift through her memories for the one that would make sense of things. And then it came at her fast and hard, slamming into her as the bullets had.

Graham.

Where was Graham?

She struggled through the drugs that hazed but didn't ease, pushing her way toward consciousness. The dark room came into focus slowly, an inch at a time and even then she wasn't entirely sure she'd succeeded in awakening. This had to be a dream.

Her father was slumped in a chair at the foot of her bed, his chin resting on his chest. The buzz of his snore sounded real, but she couldn't be sure. Her gaze caught on the hand holding hers on the thin white blanket and traveled up the arm to the side of her aunt's face illuminated by the glow of the TV playing quietly in the background. She moved her fingers, testing to see if she could touch Cerie and really be sure of what she was seeing.

Her aunt turned her head abruptly and gasped. Clasping both of Erin's hands in hers, Cerie stood and leaned over the bed.

"There you are, chicken." Cerie brushed her fingers across Erin's cheek. "We've been waiting for you to wake up." She turned and called out to her brother. "Donald. Donald!"

Erin's dad shook himself.

"She's awake," Cerie informed him.

He rushed to the other side of Erin's bed, his face creasing into a hopeful smile as he rested his hand over hers. "Hey."

"H—" Erin cleared her throat and tried again. "Hey. You're okay." She switched her attention to her aunt and then to her father again. "Both of you."

Cerie lowered the guardrail on the bed and sat on the edge, careful not to bump Erin. "We are and you will be, too."

Erin rolled her head on the pillow, needing to see Cerie's face. "Graham." She pulled in a hitching breath. "Where's Graham?"

Cerie's gaze flickered to Donald.

"I heard another shot..." Erin bit her lip, unable to finish the sentence.

"Oh, no, chicken, no. He wasn't shot."

"Then what?"

"His father died."

The cool wash of relief flooded her first, followed by the hot shame of being glad that vile, hateful man was dead. No matter what she felt about Ham, what he'd done, he'd been Graham's father. She couldn't imagine what Graham must be feeling.

"Where is he?" She wanted to see for herself that he was okay, needed to touch him to be sure.

"He was here." Donald looked over his shoulder out into the hall as though he expected to find Graham standing in the doorway.

Cerie filled in, "He's been here off and on... When he could."

"When I wasn't here," Donald said, his voice hard with anger.

"Oh, stop it," Cerie admonished. "It's not his fault. He shot his own father protecting *your* daughter. You can't seriously blame him for Ham's deeds."

Erin jerked upright, gasping at the pain slicing through her. "He *what*?"

"Lie back." Cerie gently pushed on her good shoulder. "You'll hurt yourself."

"What happened? Somebody tell me what happened."

Donald's mouth pressed down at the corners. She wasn't going to get what she wanted from her dad.

"Auntie, tell me what happened."

"First, lie back. I can see you're hurting. Let me get the nurse—"

"No." Erin put a hand on her aunt's arm to stop her from calling for the nurse. She settled back against the pillows to smooth the worry from between Cerie's brows. "I'm fine. Please. Tell me."

"A few hours after I woke up," Cerie began, "Graham came into my hospital room. I guess he'd asked the nurses to let him know when I was conscious." She paused, looking down at her hands clasped with Erin's. "He was wearing a shirt...with blood all over it. Your blood. He looked awful, chicken." She raised her gaze to Erin's, looking sadder than Erin had ever seen her. "Ham had passed right before your father and I came out of...whatever it was we were in."

Erin pressed her eyes closed. Graham shooting his own father had not only saved Erin but her aunt and dad, too. She couldn't imagine the pain he must be in right now. And blame. He'd be blaming himself for what his father had done, just like with Patricia.

"Donald arrived and then Graham told us what had happened to you," Cerie continued. "You'd just come out of surgery. You were going to be okay. And then he told us what Ham had done. He—" She broke off on a sob.

"That son of bitch nearly killed you," Donald broke in, an edge to his voice that Erin had never heard.

"I'm okay, Dad."

"You were shot. Twice."

"It's not Graham's fault."

"He's the sheriff. If it's not his fault, whose is it?"

"Donald, stop it. You're upsetting her."

"He shot his own father protecting me. And whether you like it or not, Graham and I are together. So you're just going to have to get over it."

Donald's eyes narrowed. "What do you mean *together*?"

"I mean it in the same way it applies to you and Mabel."

Cerie put a hand up to her mouth, hiding her smile.

Donald drew back. "You know about Mabel and me?"

"Mom's not coming back. You should have someone in your life who makes you happy. If that's Mabel then...that's Mabel." Her father continued to stare at her, but a strange expression crept over his features—relief. She decided to go for broke. "Daddy, I love him."

Donald looked away, his frown deepening.

"You have to let her go sometime," Cerie said to her brother. "If it helps, he loves her just as much. Maybe more. He's suffering because of what his father did. You couldn't possibly blame him as much as he blames himself. Be reasonable, Donald. He saved her at great personal cost. If you could hear him the way I do... If you knew how much pain he's in..."

"I need to see him. Please," Erin begged her aunt. "Find him for me."

"He's in the hospital, but he won't come. He..." She pressed fingers to her temples and shook her head. "I don't understand his thoughts. Something about not knowing what's real?" Cerie looked at Erin for clarification.

"Did you know about Graham's family?"

"What about them?"

"What did Ham call them?" Erin searched her memory for the right word. "Influencers. He said they were Influencers."

"What does that mean?" Donald asked.

"Oh," Cerie breathed. "He didn't know. That's why."

Donald let out a frustrated breath. "Know what?"

"That he has an ability," Erin said.

"What kind of ability?" Donald asked.

"Ham said that they're Influencers. They can influence people's thoughts and actions." Erin tried to recall everything Ham had said. "He called them crowd control. Protectors of some sort. I don't understand the details except that it has something to do with getting people to do what they want them to do."

Cerie slowly nodded. "So that's how they were able to be sheriff generation after generation."

"And why there's been no crime in San Rey," Donald added. "Until recently."

"Until Ham killed Deidre, then used his ability to influence Greg to kill himself."

"What?" Cerie and Donald said at the same time.

"It started when Ham had an affair with Deidre." Erin watched the expressions on her father's and aunt's faces go from disbelief to horror to shock as she pieced together everything Ham had done, including what had happened on the bluff. When she finished, she reached for her aunt's hand and pleaded her case one more time. "I need to see Graham, Auntie. Please."

Cerie turned to her brother, her eyes widening as her lips parted in surprise.

Donald bent and kissed Erin's forehead. "We'll leave the two of you alone." He looked at Cerie and jerked his head toward the door.

What did I miss? "What do you mean, the two of us?" Erin asked.

Cerie rose from the bed and patted Erin's hand. She smiled, her gaze on her brother's back as she leaned down to whisper in Erin's ear. "Be gentle with Graham, chicken. He's going to need your strength, but most of all he's going to need *your* ability to help him use and understand his own." She smoothed the hair back from Erin's brow. "Your father might have been a bit dramatic, putting the thought in Graham's head that he needs to get his ass up here quick. Graham's racing up and should be here in three, two, one..."

Graham suddenly appeared in the doorway. He exhaled hard when his gaze found Erin.

Cerie went to him. "Thank you for saving Erin." She patted him on the arm. "You're a good man, Graham."

GRAHAM WATCHED CERIE LEAVE, not knowing what to say, his chest still tight and heaving with the panic that he had to get to Erin. Now.

"My dad," Erin said.

Graham tried to focus on what Erin was saying, pretending he didn't see how pale and small she looked in her hospital bed. Would he ever stop seeing the image of her bleeding into the dirt? "I'm sorry." He shook his head. "What?"

"I'm all right. On the mend." She lifted a hand, the wires that hooked her to machines moving with the action. "I'm sorry if whatever thought my dad put into your head made you think otherwise."

He realized he still wasn't quite used to abilities or powers or whatever the hell they were. Maybe because he'd been suddenly handed a membership into a club he'd hardly known existed until a couple of months ago, and one he really didn't want to belong to. "He's not very happy with me."

"He'll get over it and come around. How are you?"

"Me?"

Nobody had asked him that so he didn't have a ready answer. Or any kind of answer at all. He lifted his shoulders and hoped she didn't see how badly he wanted to go to her, wrap his arms around her, and bury his face in the softness of her. She was the one thing that could ground him in the here and now, but he couldn't even walk all the way into the room with her. He stood just inside the doorway, feeling hopeless and so fucking useless, wondering why he couldn't have taken the bullets instead of her.

"I'm sorry about your father."

He flinched at her sympathy. He should be the one expressing some kind of sentiment. But what was the pat response for all the wrong Ham had inflicted? What were the words you used to smooth over the way your own father had tortured the woman you love day and night? How do you make up for using your ability to take away her free will? And what in the hell do you say to get her to look at you the way she used to?

"Come here," she beckoned softly.

Stuck in a strange, torturous limbo, he couldn't get his feet to move toward her and he couldn't leave. He'd felt nothing before, but now—here with her—he felt *everything*. His skin prickled hot and he resisted the overwhelming urge to scratch and scratch until he flayed the skin he was in and shed it for a new one that he could stand to live in.

"Graham."

She said his name in the way she used to, pulling on the string that bound them together. Except he couldn't feel the tug the way he did before, as though the line had become frayed and was dangerously close to snapping.

"It hurts," he blurted out.

"I know it does." She held her one good arm out to him and he wanted nothing more than to go to her, but he wasn't sure of what was real anymore, what was for him and what he generated without meaning to. "Come here," she offered again.

He shook his head.

"Please." She moved her fingers, inviting him in.

"No. You don't get it. You don't know."

"I know what it's like to lose a parent."

"I can't."

"Graham—"

"No! Stop it. You just don't know."

"I want to help you. I—"

"Don't you get it? It's *you*. It hurts to be with you."

She dropped her hand, her lips parting, her face growing even paler. He saw the tears forming in her eyes, but she didn't understand. He couldn't stand to be in the same room with her. It physically hurt to be near her.

And he knew it would be fucking agony to live without her.

13

"Come here," Erin said slow and even, the hard edge of anger sliding through her words. "Or I'm climbing out of this bed and coming to you."

To prove it, she flicked her covers off and started to lower her legs over the side of the bed. He was by her side in two seconds, tucking her feet back under the blankets and smoothing it down around her. She grabbed his wrist with her good hand and pulled. He had to brace himself on both sides of her hips or tumble down on top of her.

"Sit down," she ordered.

He sat. But only because she still had a grip on his wrist. And she'd been shot...and maybe because he wanted to be near her so badly he couldn't help himself.

"Lean closer so I don't have to strain myself looking up at you."

He did as she ordered, bending toward her. "Are you—"

She grabbed the back of his head and cut him off with a kiss. There was no time to react. One moment he was feeling sorry for himself, feeling guilty for her getting shot, feeling as though he didn't have the right to a place in her life, and the next he was swamped with a yearning so strong all other thought and emotion was swept away. It was just him and her and this kiss that went on and on.

She finally broke it, easing back in the bed. He found himself following her and was pulled into a one-armed hug so fierce it knocked some of the wind out of him. It wasn't her strength that surprised him, it was the way she fisted the back of his shirt, gripping him hard as though he was going to float away. Or run away.

"Don't tell me what I don't get. I *get* you. I get what you're going through. All of it. You're not walking away from me out of some misplaced sense of guilt." She jerked on his shirt. "Do you hear me?" Her voice wobbled, setting off an answering quake in the center of his chest.

He nodded and turned his face into the crook of her neck. She didn't smell like she usually did, but she felt the same and that was more than enough for him. All he wanted to do was stretch out beside her and hold her and forget.

"I thought you were dead." He could hear the tears in her voice, feel her face go hot. "I heard a gunshot..." She held him tighter. "I'm sorry. I'm so, so sorry about Ham. I can't... I don't know what to say to you." She sucked in a shaky breath and he squeezed his eyes tighter against the burning at the back of his eyes. "Thank you seems stupid. Everything I can think of is stupid and useless. Oh, god, Graham. I'm so, so sorry."

He didn't want her sympathy. All he wanted was this moment to stretch out forever. Snuggling deeper into her, he didn't answer. Being with her like this, feeling tethered in a way he'd never felt before her, it was everything he wanted and nothing of what he deserved.

"I'm the only person in this town, hell, maybe even the whole world who knows what it's like to come into an ability you don't want and don't know what to do with." She laid her cheek against his head. "Let me help you. Please. I can teach you how to use your ability and how to control it."

His throat felt as raw as the rest of him. "I don't want to use it."

"Okay. You don't have to."

"Especially not on you."

She took a deep breath and let it out slowly. "Now see, that's going to be an easy one. I already know how to block my dad and aunt. I'll just do the same with you. Actually I've been blocking you since I woke up."

He pulled back to look at her. Her lashes were wet and clumped together, her cheeks pinker than they were before. She was so goddamned beautiful his chest ached. He'd never grow tired of looking at her. Reaching up, he brushed back the lock of hair that had fallen over one eye. He wanted to believe that every-thing could be solved so simply.

"Go ahead and try," she said. "Try to use your ability."

"That's just it. I don't know how to use it. I don't even know *when* I'm using it and when I'm not."

"Close your eyes."

"There's no point."

"Just do it. For me. Please?"

He huffed out a breath and complied.

"Think about something you want me to do, raising my arm or saying a particular word. Focus your thoughts. Blank everything else out. Concentrate on what you want me to do..."

"But you're blocking me."

"For this first time I'm going to open up to you. Then we'll try it again with me blocking you."

"This isn't going to work."

"It will. Just try."

She still held onto him and he didn't ever want her to let go. So that's what he thought about, her releasing him. Taking a deep breath, he focused on her pushing him away.

Nothing.

"I told you it wouldn't work," he mumbled.

"Maybe if we aren't so close," she said, then let go of him and pushed at his chest.

He leaned back to look at her, his jaw hanging open a little. *Did that just... Did I...?* No. Couldn't be. It must be a coincidence.

"What?" she asked.

He got up and paced across the room, needing the space. It felt wrong. *He* felt wrong.

"Graham?"

"I can't do this."

"Try again. Maybe something simpler this time."

"I don't need to."

"What do you mean... *Oh*." She smiled. At what he didn't know. There was nothing to be happy about here. "Do it again."

"No."

She flipped her covers back like she was going to climb out of bed, her chin up, challenging him.

He put his hands out. "Okay. Fine. I'll try again."

"Not try...do. Do it again."

Glaring at her, he thought about her lying back and closing her eyes. She looked so damn tired. All he wanted was for her to get some rest so she could heal, instead of playing these stupid games with his ability.

Sighing, she settled back against the pillows. "One more time," she yawned. "Please? For me?"

He couldn't help the frown that bent down one side of his mouth. "You're tired. Maybe we should do this some other time."

She shook her head, blinking slowly. "I'm okay."

Returning to the side of the bed, he kissed her forehead. "No. I really think you need a nap." He started to leave.

She grabbed his wrist. "Hold it right there." Suddenly she was rebounding. Her lips pressed in a stubborn line. "You made me feel sleepy."

"This is pointless."

"You're two for two. Good job. Try it again."

"Erin—"

"I'm blocking you now. Go on. One more time and then I'll take that nap you seem to think I need."

God, she was stubborn. She wasn't going to let up on him. The sooner he complied with what she wanted him to do, the sooner she'd actually get the rest she needed.

"Fine." He imagined her telling him to fuck off, pictured her kicking him out of her hospital room, telling him she never wanted to see him again. Everything he deserved to hear. Instead all he got was a serene smile and a smug eyebrow wiggle. He frowned.

"It works," she said. "You can't use your ability on me."

"What about everyone else? They don't have the defenses you have."

"Keep practicing. You'll get better."

"I don't want to get better. I want it to go away."

"Well, that's not going to happen, is it? Do you want to accidentally use your ability or have control over it? Because those are your only two options."

He grumbled under his breath at her, knowing she was right.

Her expression softened. "How's your mom?"

Her abrupt change of subject threw him for a moment. He pulled in a tight breath. "She doesn't know yet."

"I wish I could be there with you when you tell her."

"How in the hell am I going to tell her that her son shot her husband? It'll be all over town. About him shooting you, me shooting him." Squeezing his eyes closed, he tipped his head back. "Ah, Jesus."

She took his hand in hers. "I'm so sorry."

"You don't have anything to be sorry about."

"It was because of me that your father came to the bluff."

"Don't call him that."

Erin could feel the twin chains of grief and guilt wrapped around him, squeezing and shackling him, pulling him away from her.

"It was my idea to bait him. All of it was *my* fault. Not yours. I wish I'd listened to you. If I had—"

"If you had, more people might have been hurt or died because of him. Donald and Cerie would still be suffering. None of this is your fault."

"Then it's not your fault either."

He looked away and she could tell her words had no effect.

"It was my gun," he said so low and miserable she almost didn't hear him.

She wished to God she hadn't. His words hit like a punch in the gut, knocking the wind out of her. She could hardly catch her breath. So this was it. This would be the thing that would tear them apart. She couldn't fight through the blame he cloaked himself in.

Just like Patricia.

Was he here now out of some kind of penance? If they managed to stay together, would she ever really know if it was what he wanted or if he was trying to atone for the wrongs he thought he'd inflicted on her? She could imagine it. Every day like the lash of a whip, marking off his punishment. When would it end for him? What would happen to them if she let him go on carrying the burden for what his father had done and his accidental role in it?

"I'm going to tell you something you're not going to believe. You're not going to believe it because you're one of the most responsible, honest people I've ever met. And you're stubborn, so freaking stubborn." She had his attention, however reluctant. Fat lot of good it would do her. "So here it is... *It's not your fault.* Ham picking up your gun and shooting me... Not your fault. It's Ham's. He started this whole tragedy and wouldn't have given up until it played out the way he wanted. He left you no choice. You ended his reign of terror and horror. You saved me. You saved who knows how many other people. As far as I'm concerned you're a hero."

His wince at the word 'hero' made her want to grab him and shake him, but she knew it wouldn't do any good. She could tell him a thousand times in a thousand ways that none of this was his fault. Her words would only bounce off him, deflected by his self-imposed torment. He'd been as swept up into the current of Ham's manipulations and evilness as the rest of them. But her telling him such wouldn't do any good. He had to discover it for himself.

She itched to look into the future to see if he would ever realize it or to find the one thing that would bring him around. But that wouldn't be right and above all else she wanted her relationship with Graham to be honest. So she'd do the hard thing. She wouldn't look into the future, she wouldn't manipulate him, and she'd tear her own heart out before she ever let him look at her again the way he was looking at her now.

"I won't be an...obligation to you," she stuttered out. "I want you, but not with you thinking you owe me or trying to make up for what your father did. You can't fix it and you can't undo it. It's done."

"You're not an obligation."

"What then? What am I to you other than a living symbol of all the ways you think you've failed?"

"I have no idea what you mean." He denied it, but she could see him scrambling inside, looking for a way to make things right.

"I've become Patricia to you."

"What in the hell are you talking about?"

"You know what I'm talking about. I can absolve you eight ways to Sunday, but until you forgive yourself we have nowhere to go."

"So you're what? Breaking up with me?"

"I'm freeing you of your obligation."

"What the fuck is that supposed to mean?"

She bowed her head and rubbed her eyes. So tired. She was so tired and achy, hurting from the inside out. "I can't be the amends you make. I can't be the thing that ties you to this town. I can't let you use our relationship as some kind of half-assed attempt at absolution."

"That's not—"

She whipped her head up to glare at him. "Bullshit!"

"I don't know what you think you know about me, but you're all wrong."

"Am I?"

No, she wasn't, Graham suddenly realized. Not entirely. Her tone was like a chisel to his chest, chipping away at all the bullshit she'd called him out on. He *did* feel guilty for her getting shot. It *was* his fault. The bullets he'd loaded into his gun had torn through her flesh and could've killed her.

Everything was so fucked up and off center he couldn't entirely trust his own judgment when it came to her. She'd gotten one important fact wrong though —he was so head over heels in love with her he hardly had a thought without her in it. And he definitely didn't see her as an obligation.

"You're not tying me to this town." It was all he had to offer her. "I'm the sheriff. At least I will be once I'm cleared and off of administrative leave. With Adam away I'm all my mom's got. I've been planning on staying in San Rey for some time now."

She laughed, but it rang hollow and sad between them. "Really? That's a switch."

"What do you want me to say?" Because he'd say it, do it, whatever it took to make her stay with him.

"Nothing."

"So that's it? We're just over."

"Yeah, I guess so."

She stared at him, hugging her disappointment to her as tightly as her arm wrapped around her body. Goddammit! What did she want from him?

He turned and left, his feet taking him away from

her and the purest moments of joy he'd ever known. The further he got, the hotter he burned. By the time he exited the hospital he wanted to hit something so bad he shook with it. He climbed into his car and slammed the door closed. Tearing out of the parking lot, he didn't care about getting lit up for speeding. He had to get far away from Erin and her words that chased him like rabid dogs, chomping and snarling.

He struck the steering wheel with the flat of his hand over and over until the pain radiated up his arm and into his shoulder. It didn't help. The pressure rose inside, threatening to spill over.

What in the hell was he supposed to do without her?

14

Erin was released from the hospital the same day as Ham's funeral. She sat at the back of the church with her aunt who had insisted on coming along with her even though Cerie would rather spit on Ham's casket than grieve over it.

Erin wasn't there to mourn Ham either. There were no respects to pay. She wasn't sure why she'd come. Maybe it was for a glimpse of Graham, to see how he was doing and to be there for him in some small way. They'd slipped into the end of the last pew just before the service started so all she could see of him was the back of his head. He had an arm across his mother's shaking shoulders and would lean down to whisper to her every now and then.

Erin accepted the well wishes of passersby. Their concern felt genuine as though she was truly, finally one of them. The tale of what had happened between her and Graham and Ham had somehow become romanticized, like some twisted Romeo and Juliet tale.

The townspeople accepted it as a point of town pride and there'd been talk about some kind of plaque or monument to what had happened on the bluffs, which she'd heard Graham had quashed.

If they only knew the true story.

The service began and the reverend spoke of Ham's accomplishments, his tenure as sheriff, his family, and his community activities. There was no mention of the deaths he'd caused or the terror he'd inflicted. Nearly the entire town of San Rey had turned out. Every seat was filled, with the overflow standing at the sides and back. And not one of them had any idea that the man they'd come to pay tribute to was a monster.

The mayor made a speech, followed by a few community leaders. Then Graham rose and made his way to the front of the room. Her stomach whooshed at her first sight of him since that day in the hospital. She'd heard that he'd been cleared in the shooting and reinstated as sheriff. She was glad. He didn't deserve to pay for what his father had done.

He wore a somber dark suit and tie, which hung like it had been made for him. He looked out at the crowd through tired eyes. She drank him in, savoring every single nuance, from the way he'd combed his hair back to the new lines that bracketed his mouth. Had it only been a little over a week since she'd seen him? It felt like forever.

"My mother, brother, and I would like to thank you all for coming," he began. "In lieu of flowers, we're asking for donations to The Alzheimer's Foundation of

America. Your support through this difficult time for our family means the world to us. Thank you."

As he turned from the podium his gaze caught on Erin, lingered, then swung away toward his mother. She'd almost forgotten what it felt like to have Graham Doran's attention on her. It still packed a punch that would've rocked her back on her heels if she'd been standing. She wanted to go to him and offer comfort, but it wasn't her place anymore.

"It'll be all right, chicken." Aunt Cerie bumped Erin's shoulder, her voice barely above a whisper. "He'll come around. If it's any consolation, he's pining away for you. When he saw you he thought—"

Erin held up a hand. "I don't want to know his thoughts. Please don't eavesdrop on him. Graham's off limits."

"He knows I'm listening. He's worried about you."

"What part off *he's off limits* do you not understand?"

Cerie fluttered a hand. "Fine. Fine. Have it your way. But I think you should give the man another chance."

"What is or isn't happening between Graham and me is none of your business."

The service ended and everyone stood. Erin watched as Graham went to the front corner of his father's casket and hefted it up with the other pallbearers. They slowly made their way down the aisle while the church organ moaned. Graham stared straight ahead, his back rigid. As he passed, Erin couldn't resist reaching out and brushing his hand, a silent show of support. To her surprise he grabbed her fingers, giving them the briefest squeeze, before dropping them and moving out into the gray morning.

Erin held her breath, barely managing to stifle a sob. She knew she'd done the right thing for both of them, but the right thing was never the easiest. Unable to tear her gaze from his retreating back, she slipped out after the family and stood to the side at the top of the church steps as the rest of the mourners filed out past her.

Cerie slipped her hand into Erin's and hugged her arm. "He's holding up well. Maybe better than you."

"I didn't think it would be so hard to see him and not be with him."

"He's carrying a burden bigger and heavier than his father's casket."

"I wish I knew how to help him."

"Give him some time. He'll come around."

"I hope you're right."

GRAHAM SET Ham's casket on the metal rails at the back of the hearse and helped slide it in. He'd gone through all the motions of being a good son, doing everything expected of him, and now there was just one more thing to do—lay Ham to an easier rest than he deserved.

He helped his mother into his car and then climbed in on the driver's side. He'd spent the week making funeral arrangements and making sure she was properly cared for by hiring a nurse and moving into the house with her. Tomorrow he'd start back to work as sheriff of San Rey. He was surprised at how much he looked forward to it. Maybe the day-to-day of police work would distract him from thoughts of Erin, thoughts he'd finally gotten a handle on until he'd seen her in the church.

He'd done a pretty good job of putting up a front and focusing on what needed to be done to get through this day. He saw her and his head got so crowded with everything they'd been and done together, he could hardly breathe. And then she'd touched him and he had to focus hard on getting out the door and down the stairs, each step away from her a pounding reminder of how much he'd let her down.

"That was a lovely service," his mother said. "Who was it for?"

Her question caught him off guard. Again. This would be the third time he'd have to tell her that her husband was dead. When they'd arrived at the church and she saw the portrait of Ham beside his casket, she'd broken down, beginning the grieving process as though it was the first time. He could shatter her world all over again now or wait until they got to the gravesite when she'd see the temporary headstone and the horrific shock would grip her anew once more.

So he lied and told her that the funeral was for an old church friend of hers who'd died several years ago.

"Oh, no," she gasped. "Her poor family. Did we send flowers?"

"Yes, Ma."

"Such a shame. I'm sure going to miss her blueberry pie."

Everyday seemed to bring new punctures in her memory, so it was strange the things that would stick—like blueberry pie. Her memories spun on a roulette wheel with no way of knowing on what time of her life the ball would stop. His mother would be caught in the cycle of forgetting Ham's death, then mourning her husband all over again for the rest of her life. He didn't know how many more times he could watch her go through it. She'd truly loved her husband. They'd had a good marriage. Or so everyone had assumed.

And then for some reason Ham had taken up with Deidre and everything had gone to shit. He'd had some time to think through the whys of what Ham had done. Spending so much time with his mother, he began to see how much her illness must have changed their relationship. Still, how had things gotten to where Ham had stepped outside their marriage? That alone was so unlike Ham, almost more than the killing.

He glanced at his mother who had taken out the knitting she always carried with her and was now happily working her yarn as though she wasn't on her way to bury her husband. Maybe she was better off than the rest of them. Her world stayed calm until reality intruded and she'd have to face all the things her mind had hidden from her with no choice but to go through tragedies over and over again.

Stuck. She was stuck within the prison of her own mind, never moving forward, never fully present. Hadn't Erin accused him of the same thing, of being stuck in a cycle of guilt and obligation that had no end? He couldn't make amends for what Ham had done. He knew that. He did. Although he was having a hard time working through his role in what had happened, he was beginning to learn how to live with it and beat back all the could have's and should have's of that night.

Erin had called him a hero. He was no hero. Careless. He'd been so fucking careless with the people in his life. No more. He'd worked hard in the past few days at breaking that pattern and was finally beginning to feel like he was accomplishing something in caring for his mother. She wasn't an obligation. He was actually getting pretty good at gauging her moods. He'd learned how to redirect her when she became fixated on something and worked herself into exhaustion, worrying about things that didn't exist anymore or weren't hers to worry about.

And that first time when redirecting didn't work, he'd been forced to use his ability to calm his mother down. It had worked. He knew it would but still, using it that first time was like learning to rush in as a first responder when every survival instinct he had screamed at him to get out.

The nights were the worst for his mother. He'd stand outside her bedroom door and will her to settle down and go to sleep until he heard her soft snores. She'd reward him in the morning with pancakes as if he was on summer vacation or home from college for the holidays. It was almost like being mothered by her all over again. No, not an obligation. Not an obligation at all.

Maybe caring for his mother and fully embracing his role as sheriff was its own kind of absolution, of making wrongs right because he was in a position to do so and not out of guilt. He was even beginning to enjoy and depend on small town life. There was a certain peaceful ebb and flow to it as predictable as the ocean tides. Neighbors had volunteered to help him with his mother and brought them so much food he'd filled up his mother's refrigerator *and* the one at the station. He'd had to learn to accept the help, to smile and say thank you, knowing when his neighbors needed him, he'd be there for them.

He finally felt as though he belonged here, in this smallest of small towns. Who could've predicted that?

The only glaring hole in his life was the one Erin should've filled. As he drove into the cemetery near the plot where Ham—no, his father, he couldn't run away from that anymore—would finally come to rest, he made a vow to convince Erin some way, somehow that he *was* indeed finally the man she'd challenged him to be.

15

The sea threw its all at the rocks, crashing in big booms, shooting sheets of spray straight up, misting Erin from head to toe. Not that it mattered, with the sky doing its best to outdo the ocean. Lightning flashed, followed shortly by thunder. She wasn't sure why she'd come here. Certainly it was foolish in such bad weather. Her hair hung in limp ropes and her wet clothes clung, chilling her. She welcomed the idea that the rain could somehow wash away what had happened in this place nearly a month ago.

This was the first time she'd dared to venture out here. Recapturing her favorite place in San Rey—in the whole world, really—felt like the last step she needed to banish the nightmares for good. Sure, she could've come up here to the bluffs on a sunny afternoon, but where was the challenge in that? She laughed at herself. She'd been such a scared little mouse most of her life and now here she was, pushing herself, braving the elements to prove the point to herself that she could be bold and daring.

She raised her arms and tilted her head toward the sky. The twinge in her shoulder barely registered beyond the cold that had seeped into her bones. Another few weeks of physical therapy and she'd be pronounced whole once again. Other than the scars on her body, there would be nothing left of that night. She smiled to herself at that. She'd done it. She'd fought the monster and her own demons and had come out the other side stronger, if not happier.

"It's good to see you like this."

She lowered her arms, but didn't spin around. Somehow she knew he'd come or he'd known she would come. Either way, here they were.

She turned around slowly, bracing herself to see him up close for the first time in weeks. Her preparation was wasted. Nothing could've prepared her for the sight of him as wet as she, standing just a few feet away.

"It's good to feel like this," she answered.

He cocked his head to the side, a small smile tilting up one corner of his mouth. "Nice weather we're having."

She tucked her hands in her coat pockets and gave him the same sort of smile in return. "Isn't it?"

"I've heard if you count one-Mississippi, two-Mississippi after a lightning strike, you can tell how close a storm is. Four-Mississippi would be four miles away."

"Is it important to you to know how far away a storm is?"

"It's important for me to know where I stand in nature. It can turn on a dime."

She nodded. "Hmm, I've heard that. Do you think by predicting how far away a storm is that you can know for certain when it will reach you?"

"Maybe. If I've done all the right things in the right way for the right reasons." He looked up at the sky as lightning flashed. "One-Mississippi, two-Mississippi, three-Mississippi, four-Mississip—"

In four short steps she crashed into him. They held each other hard as though the storm would sweep them out to sea. She tilted her face up, he met her halfway, and they kissed a slow, winding kiss that spun her world on its axis. It had been so long since she'd been with him. So long since she'd felt him, *so long* since the scent of him wrapped around her.

Holding her face in his hands, he broke the kiss and stared down at her. "They also say that storms wash everything clean. Do you believe that?"

"I think that's quite possible, depending on how strong it is."

"What about one as strong as this one?"

She glanced up as another flash of light streaked the sky. "One-Mississippi, two-Miss—" Thunder roared.

Graham's heart beat nearly as loud as the thunder. "It's almost on top of us."

She nodded, her face sliding through his fingers, wet from the rain and her tears.

"I'm not leaving until it's right on top of us," he promised.

"Me either."

"We can keep counting as it moves on, track its progress."

"I don't think I can stay here that long."

"No?"

She shook her head. "I don't need to. I'll believe you when you tell me the worst is over."

Relief washed through him. "I can do that."

The sky blazed bright, illuminating them for a split second.

"One-Miss," they whispered together.

BOOM.

"It's here," she breathed.

Bringing her face to his chest, needing that full body connection, he held her tighter. "I've got you."

The rain came down at them sideways, pelting them with heavy drops. All around them, a wall of sound and sensation made it seem as if they were the last two people on earth.

"And I've got you." She gripped his back and held on just as tight.

The thunderstorm raged as though it had gained new strength and purpose. The sea seemed to try to raise itself to meet it, the waves more violent than they'd been before. But for Graham there was only the two of them in this place that had been so many things to them—where they'd first come together, where they'd nearly lost each other, and now where they'd finally found each other again.

He slowly came to notice that the rain had let up. In the distance the thunder rumbled, signaling the all clear. He dared to pull away a little to look down at her. He couldn't wrap his mind around the fact that she was finally here in his arms again.

ERIN BLINKED UP AT HIM, needing to be sure she wasn't seeing things in the rain. It was gone, that heavy lidded look of remorse he'd had. She couldn't help the joy that coursed through her. He'd finally come back to her, finally forgiven himself and cut loose the weighty ties of grief and guilt.

"I love you," she blurted out.

He stilled. Even his breathing seemed to be suspended as he stared at her through the darkness.

"It's okay, Graham. You don't have to say or do anything. I just wanted you to know."

"Why?" he whispered with a faint note of disbelief.

"I don't know. I just do. I mean, how do you explain—"

He put a finger to her lips, silencing her. "I don't care why."

She pulled his hand away, annoyed. "Then why did you ask?"

"Because I can't imagine why you would." He kissed her hard and quick. "But I really don't care why. I'm just so damn grateful."

"Okay." Not the response she'd expected. At least he hadn't thanked her.

"Thank you."

Fantastic. "You're welcome... I guess." This wasn't going quite as she'd thought it would.

"No. That's not what I...I mean..." He put his forehead to hers. "Thank god you love me too."

"Yeah?"

"Yeah."

"Thank you."

He laughed. "You're welcome."

"Now what?"

"Now I take you home and show you just how much I love every single inch of you."

*

Thank you for reading RARE! The next book in the DANGEROUS LINES series is BETRAY.

Gia did something a spy should never do—she fell in love with her target.

➤CLICK HERE TO READ BETRAY➤

If you enjoyed RARE, please consider leaving a review on your favorite book site. Reviews help readers find books!

➤RARE (DANGEROUS LINES novel)➤

➤GOODREADS➤

Join my VIP Facebook group Babes with Books for exclusive sneak peeks at my upcoming books & other, members only, perks:

➤www.facebook.com/groups/BabesWithBooks-ReaderGroup

Sign up to receive my newsletter for new release alerts, exclusive bonus content, and giveaways!

➤**www.bethyarnall.com/newsletter**

Turn the page to read an excerpt from BETRAY now! ☞

EXCERPT FROM BETRAY

I bolted awake, jackknifing upright.

I'd had this dream before. It always ended with him finding me. No matter where I ran or how well I hid, he *always* tracked me down. Sometimes the chase would go on and on and sometimes it was over almost before it started. Knowing I had no chance of escape, I still ran. I ran and ran and ran until I woke up drenched in sweat, my heart beating out a marathon runner's pace.

This time was no different.

Heart pounding in my ears, I blinked hard, rubbing my eyes and trying to bring the room into focus. My vision sharpened, but the outline of the man didn't fade. No. It couldn't be.

"Good morning, Glory."

That voice. My nightmare come to life.

Fear slammed into me a second time. Digging my heels into the mattress, I pushed myself as far back in the bed as I could.

"Where are you going?" He laughed, his voice unexpectedly rough and accusing. "I told you I'd be back." He made no move, yet his tone made my body freeze up.

I heard the strike a split second before the match lit his face, then extinguished. The room filled with the scent of fine tobacco. His scent. I swallowed the bile rising at the back of my throat.

"Did you think I wouldn't find you? I admit you gave me a chase. Changing your name, your looks. I liked that you made it difficult. A man appreciates a good hunt." He rose from the chair, but made no move toward me. Instead he walked to the dresser and picked up a framed photo.

"Who is he?" he asked with a calmness that made the hair at the nape of my neck prickle. I could feel his stare on me through the dimly lit room, an undeniable force. "Glory." His volume and tenor were unchanged yet I started at the sound of his pet name for me.

"A friend," I answered in measured tones.

"A friend." He dropped the photo, shattering the glass against the hardwood floor. "Am I not your friend, Glory?" His voice took on a new calmness that frightened me even more.

Pressed up hard against the headboard, I cautiously told him what I thought he wanted to hear. "Yes."

"Hmm." He seemed to consider my answer as he sucked hard on his cigarette, making it glow hot in the early-morning darkness. He strolled to the other side of the room and picked up the black dress I'd discarded earlier in the evening. He rubbed it between his fingers then pressed it to his face, inhaling deeply. "The smell of you, that is unchanged." He turned toward me slowly. "I can smell you from here, Glory." The suggestiveness in his voice scattered goose bumps over my body.

I watched him with all the wariness of a fly trapped in a spider's web.

He threw the dress at me. "Put it on."

"What?"

"Really, Glory. You're caught. Do you not realize this?" He relaxed back into the chair he'd occupied earlier, propping his ankle on his knee. "Put. It. On." He took a hard drag then ground his cigarette out on the bottom of his shoe.

I debated going against him, but old memories had me quickly wriggling out of my nightgown and into the evening dress under the cover of the darkened room. Never taking my eyes off his shadowy shape, I adjusted the dress as best I could.

"Stand."

I did as I was told, scrambling off the far side of the bed.

"Turn the light on."

I panicked, taking a step back.

"Glory, my patience has an end," he warned.

Taking a breath, I clicked on the bedside lamp, illuminating my face then my body as I straightened to face him.

"Madre de Dios," he hissed, bolting out of his chair. He surged forward, forcing me against the window. The cold from the windowpane seeped through the curtains to my skin. He gripped my arm, shaking me. "What have you done?"

A new boldness brought my chin up, and for the first time I let all the anger and helplessness he'd burdened me with for most of my adult life seep out as defiance. "What does it look like?"

He struck my face hard, knocking me to the floor. His kick sent me into the wall. I'd been dealt these blows before... and more.

"You stupid, bitch." He yanked me up by the front of my dress, his face inches from mine, and in the lamp-light I saw something I'd never seen before. Fear. Real fear. He shook me again, rattling my head like a rag doll.

"Careful, Carlos. You wouldn't want to hurt the baby."

He released me, staring at the twist in the front of my dress just above my gently rounded belly, horror turning his face pale. This close, I could smell the stench of panicked sweat, mingling with his fine Mexican tobacco. I hadn't expected his reaction. If I had, I would have handled his return much differently.

He stepped back slowly, edging his way around the bed toward the door, watching me all the while. I stayed where I was, sensing my new vulnerability was the impetus for his escape.

I took my first real gulp of air as he disappeared through the doorway.

I broke into tears at the click of the front door closing behind him.

*

Want to read more?

➤One-click BETRAY Now➤

If you loved RARE, you'll love the sexy, funny, award nominated INNOCENT serial. Cora's brother was convicted of a murder he didn't commit and it's up to her to set him free. Inspired by real cases taken on by The Innocence Project.

★ Nominated in 2017 for the Romance Writers of America Rita® award★

➤One-click EPISODE ONE Now➤

Looking for something lighter and funny? Check out THE MISADVENTURES OF MAGGIE MAE series, starting with WAKE UP, MAGGIE, available now! Maggie has to keep her very inappropriate thoughts to herself about the FBI Special Agent assigned to protect her from a murderer.

➤One-click WAKE UP, MAGGIE Now➤

ALSO BY BETH YARNALL

Dangerous Lines

Lost

Saved

Fake

Real

Urge

Rare

Betray

Recovered Innocence

Liberate

Exonerate

Vindicate

Innocent Serial

Episode One

Episode Two

Episode Three

The Misadventures of Maggie Mae

Wake Up, Maggie

You're Mine, Maggie

Find Me, Maggie

Azalea March Mysteries

Dyed and Gone

Beth Writing as Betty Paper

Exposed

Captive

Tinsel

Piano Lessons

BETH'S BOOKS FOR WRITERS

Crafting Unputdownable Fiction series

Going Deep Into Deep Point of View

Making Description Work Hard For You

Some Like It Hot: Writing Sex and Romance

ACKNOWLEDGMENTS

I could not have finished this book without the support and encouragement of my local Romance Writers of America chapter—OCC/RWA. You are the rockingest group of writers in the world. My critique partners Debra Mullins, Charity Hammond, and Alison Diem cheered me on when the writing days were bleak and the urge to quit was strong. You're the duct tape that kept me together while writing this book. Many thanks to my mom and sister who are the last set of eagle eyes to read my books before they go to print. Any mistakes are totally their fault not mine. *Muchas gracias* to the guys in my life—my dad, husband, and sons—your support means the world to me. We're just that most closer to a swimming pool boys.

ABOUT THE AUTHOR

USA Today best selling author and Rita® finalist, Beth Yarnall, writes mysteries, romantic suspense, and the occasional hilarious tweet. She lives in Southern California with her husband, two sons, and their rescue dogs where she is hard at work on her next novel. For more information about Beth and her novels please visit her website- www.bethyarnall.com

facebook.com/bethyarnallauthor

amazon.com/author/bethyarnall

bookbub.com/authors/beth-yarnall